1

Novels in the Trilogy relating to Diya

Loved to Death

Loved to Hell

Loved to Paradise

Loved to Valhalla

The Ladies

Flora

Blood Moon

Diya

Written By Linda Larson

Chapter 1

Diya was born in the fields with the dew still on the leaves of the plants that surrounded her . The earth was still fresh and the skies bluer then the brightest blue . She never knew when or what date she was born on , it was before any records were kept . Her mother had told her that when she gave birth the sun had came over the hills like a lamp spreading gods love so she named her Diya .

Her mother was a simple woman who never spoke much . She would wrap up Diya everyday and go work in the fields . As Diya grew she would follow behind her mother in her footsteps as they walked . They lived in a small wooden cabin deep in the forest , huge trees surrounded them like a fortress . It was a enchanted place to Diya and she would often just sit in the forest to listen to its sounds .

Her mother taught her many things as she grew . Diya knew how to hunt and fish , She also knew how to sew , clean and even braid her own hair . Diya listened closely when her mother talked and was a quick learner . Her mother would never praise her nor would she ever anger . Her mother seemed more like a care taker . A hug was a very rare thing . When Diya would ask her mother her real name but she would just reply mother .

They would get down on their knees every morning to pray , it was the closest that Diya ever felt to her mother as they would kneel next to each other . Diya would repeat every word as her mother spoke , even though she did not understand the words she wanted her mother to be proud .

They would light a piece of wood and offer it to the gods along with any food they had .

Diya did not understand why her mother would give gods food when she had barely any . If they were gods, wouldn't they have all the food they needed ? Her mother assured her they did but offering their food would protect them from all evil . Diya did not see this evil that her mother spoke of and would sometimes sneak out and eat the food left out for the gods . She did not want to anger her mother but she figured the gods would be happier if she had a full belly .

They had no family or friends . Diya would question her mother as to why they were alone , her mother would remain silent as if that was all the answer the Diya needed .

Once a month they would walk to the nearest village . Her mother would always trade for the things they needed . Diya would stare at the people , holding on to her mothers dress tightly . She loved their village trips , her eyes always wide with amazement of all the different things . The villagers were always nice and sometimes would

offer Diya toys or treats. Before Diya could say yes
her mother would always say no . The villagers
would give her a sad look but obey her mothers
wishes .

Diya found a friend in the forest
one day . She was chasing a white rabbit through
the brush . It weaved back and forth around the
trees but Diya was fast and nimble and kept up to
the little rabbit . She was reaching out to grab its
ears when she tripped on a tree root . Diya went
crashing into the forest ground , hitting her head
as she fell . Her lungs would not work at first and
as Diya gasped for breath she saw it .

A black little creature floating in the
air . It had little wings holding its little furry body
afloat. Little fuzzy paws to match its little fuzzy
head . It was the cutest creature Diya had ever
seen . It was peeking at Diya from behind a tree
barely making a sound . As the air filled Diya's
lungs, she sat frozen on the ground watching
the little thing as it continued to watch her .

Diya did a soft whistle as if to call the creature closer . It remained unmoving , hovering in one spot . Diya pulled out a piece of bread and placed it on the ground next to her , she then closed her eyes and waited . Minutes went by and Diya tired of waiting opened her eyes to discover the bread gone . Looking up she could see the creature was hovering in the same place but now was eating the piece of bread .

This continued for weeks . Diya would show up and leave pieces of bread on the ground and close her eyes . Every time she reopened her eyes the bread would gone and the little creature would appear with bread in paws . Then one day she opened her eyes and there it was ! Sitting on the ground next to her . Diya put her hand out and it tenderly put its paw out to touch . They sat there for hours just staring at each other . As the afternoon ended , Diya sadly got up to return home . Walking away she looked back and the creature was already gone .

The next day Diya returned to the spot , looking around she could not see her fuzzy little friend . She took out a piece of bread and left it on the ground and closed her eyes . To her surprise this time when she opened her eyes , there was not one creature but two of them now . The new creature was a brilliant white color and just as curious as the first one, if not more , it wasted no time and flew right up to Diya's face and poked her in the nose . Diya giggled , it was as if a cloud had touched her . The creature flew back hearing the giggles as if confused by the unknown sound . The black creature would eat the bread and the white creature examined Diya like she was the unknown creature . Diya did not mind , she rather liked the attention . This went on for weeks . Diya was overjoyed to not have one friend but now two .

One evening Diya grew brave and asked her mother about such flying creatures in the forest , explaining them in detail . Her mothers eyes went wide and then she got angry . She forbid Diya from going to the forest claiming they were dangerous evil spirits , not real . Diya knew they were real and not spirits . She had never seen her mother mad before and wondered why she would be so mad over these cute little creatures . Her mother said they were called Floras and they were not to be trusted .

" Floras " whispered Diya .

Diya did not understand her mothers anger and agreed to not going to see them again , even though she knew it was a lie .

The next day Diya had a hard time not running to see her new friends . She did as always , sitting in the same place and leaving out a piece of bread . She closed her eyes and counted to 10 . Diya opened her eyes and gasped . There were Floras everywhere ! Hundreds of them flying above her head in circles , others sitting on the ground next to her , in the trees , they were everywhere . Diya stood up and turned in circles laughing . It was the most beautiful thing she had ever seen .

One of the Floras flew up to Diya and said Hello and then flew away . She stood speechless , they talk ?

" Hello ? " said Diya quietly .

" Hello " replied a dozen Floras at the same time .

" Boo ! " said Diya louder this time .

" BOO " yelled the same dozen Floras .

They were copying her ! She started to laugh again and sat back down on the ground watching the Floras .

As weeks went by Diya snuck to the forest as often as she could . She no longer needed bread or to close her eyes to summon the Floras , she just needed to give a whistle and some would show up within minutes . Diya would spend hours playing hide and seek with her new friends . The Floras would bring her little trinkets to play with and keep .

One night one of the trinkets

14

fell out of her pocket as she sat on her bed . It fell

on the floor , the noise it made as it hit the floor

echoed in the little cabin . Her mother ran over and

picked up the trinket examining it closely . It was a

little bronze horse , maybe a inch long . One of

Diya's favorites , carved in such detail the little

horse almost seemed alive .

Her mother grew angry and walked

over to the fire throwing her miniature horse into

it . Diya screamed out loud . Her mother turned

and grabbed the broom , she started hitting Diya

while screaming she had been touched by evil .

Chapter 2

Diya awoke the next morning to a knock at the door . Her eyes wide she watched as her mother opened it and let in a stranger . He had to bend over as he entered the cabin . The stranger was as tall as the trees wearing a long black cloak . He talked with her mother for a few minutes and then he gave her a pile of money . She pointed at Diya .

He walked over and held his hand out . Diya just sat and looked at it .

" Go ! " said her mother pointing out the door .

" Come " said the stranger .

Diya went to back up on her bed and the stranger bent over and picked her up with

16

ease , as if she weighed nothing more then a feather . Surprised Diya sat in his arms as he left the cabin and her mother behind , she watched her mother in the doorway as the man carried her further away with every step . Her mother did not shed a tear or even say goodbye .

He walked in silence , carrying Diya . He walked for just over a hour and came to a horse tied to a tree . It was a huge horse and seemed happy with his return . He set Diya down on the ground .

" Do not go anywhere " said the man as he untied the horse from the tree .

Diya stood patiently and watched the man . He turned and picked her up , set her on the horse and then soon joined her .

" Hold on we have a journey ahead of us " said the man as he pulled on the horses reins and gave it a kick . The horse eager to go shot off like a bullet across the field . Diya looked back at the forest and teared up , her Floras , she

17

would never see her friends again . She quickly
wiped the tears from her eyes and looked ahead .
Soon they went past the furthest she had ever been
in her little bit of life . The man stared ahead
concentrating on the terrain .

They rode for hours and then
stopped at a river . The horse needed water and
rest . The man took Diya down from the horse .

" Stay here " said the man pointing
to the ground as if to make his point .

Diya did as told . The man was not
gone long and returned with a rabbit . She watched
as he made a fire , skinned the rabbit and cooked
it . It smelt wonderful and Diya was hungry . He
took it from the fire and cut it up , using a rock as
a table . He motioned for her to come and eat . Diya
ran over and grabbed a piece of the rabbit and
started eating .

" Hungry little one you are " said
the man in between bites .

It was the best rabbit Diya had

ever ate .

" Do you talk ? " asked the man .

Diya just looked at the man . She could talk but did not want to talk to him . He was different . This man did not look like her mother or anyone she had ever seen before . he was a pale white skin with blue eyes , long dark straight air hung down past his shoulders .

" Your mother said you could talk " said the man looking at Diya . He got up and grabbed Diya , walking over to the river he hung her upside down over the flowing water , holding onto her one leg . She screamed .

" Can you talk ? " asked the man calmly .

Diya stopped screaming and remained silent . He lowered her until the top of her head was in the river . She could see the water rushing towards her , she had never been in water before and did not know how to swim . He started to swing her back and forth .

" One " said the man swinging her back and forth .

" Stop ! " yelled Diya suddenly as she started crying .

" Oh , so you do speak and understand me " said the man as he put Diya on the ground softly .

Diya got herself up and walked back to the fire .

" I am Rion " said the man .

" I am Diya " said Diya .

" Listen , we have a long way to travel and I do not want any grief from you . If you try and run I will find you , so don't mess around ok ? " said Rion with a serious look on his face .

Diya nodded and looked back at the fire .

" How long ? " asked Diya.

"Over 100 days " answered Rion.

" Ok " said Diya .

" You are a smart little girl , get

some sleep princess " said Rion as he sat down beside the fire .

" I am NOT a princess ! " said Diya as she turned her back . She soon fell asleep , using a bundle of grass for a pillow .

Diya woke up to the horse licking her face , she broke out in a smile .

" Good morning horse " said Diya giggling .

" Good morning girl " said Rion .

Diya nodded in response and Rion laughed . He picked her up and put her on the horse and jumped on . The horse was ready for another days travel . It was like the day before , they rode for hours then would have a break , then ride until it grew dark . This happened everyday . Sometimes they would find a little settlement , stay for a night and then leave again . Rion would tell people Diya was his daughter and they were traveling home . Diya would not argue , she had always wanted a dad and hoped they were indeed traveling home . They rode a lot in silence , Diya learned to trust Rion more and more as everyday passed .

They spent over 150 days on their journey before Diya spoke to Rion directly .

" Are we almost home ? " asked Diya .

" Oh the girl speaks " said Rion .

Diya nodded her head in response .

" Yes girl we are almost to your home " answered Rion .

" My home ? I thought I was staying with you ? " said Diya surprised .

" I have no home girl " answered Rion .

" But , I want to stay with you " said Diya sadly .

" No girl , I am just delivering you " said Rion firmly .

" To who ? " asked Diya .

" I don't know " said Rion .

" I am scared " said Diya .

" You shouldn't be " said Rion .

" Why ? " asked Diya.

" Girl you are what six years of
age ? " asked Rion .

" Yes " answered Diya not really
sure .

" Someone paid me to go and gather
you , and travel over six thousand miles to bring
you back . You are important . I don't know why . I
am not paid to know why . " explained Rion .

They traveled another couple days
before the country side changed completely . Diya
had gotten used to wide open spaces and very few
people . As they got closer to her destination she
noticed the buildings were huge and made out of
brick . There were people everywhere , horses and
guard's .

" What is this ? " asked Diya .

" This is Rome " answered Rion .

" Rome " whispered Diya .

23

The country side turned into a city before Diya's eyes . The road went from gravel to cobblestone . There were many businesses with many people walking around . As they neared the center of town Diya could see a huge structure , like a big bowl . It was lit up and had over a thousand people in it . They were cheering loudly .

Diya's mind was on overload , she leaned back into Rion as he made her feel safe . They stopped suddenly and Rion jumped off of the horse . They were in front of a church . It was the biggest building Diya had ever seen . It had a huge cross on the top of it and windows that had color in them . The doors were made of wood and had carved pictures on them . Everything looked really old , much older then Diya was . Rion came out of the building and picked up Diya off of the horse to put her down on the ground . She followed him up the steps and through the wooden doors . The inside of the church glowed gold almost blinding Diya with its intensity .

Her eyes adjusted and she was amazed at how beautiful the inside of the church was . Angels were drawn on the walls , the isles were so clean and people were sitting on the benches praying .

" This is her ? " asked a lady as she came down the isle towards Diya and Rion .

" Yes " replied Rion .

" Does she speak ? " asked the lady bending over to look at Diya .

" Yes , when she wants to " answered Rion chuckling .

" Hello , my name is Rose " said the lady .

Chapter 3

Rose took Diya's hand and walked her through the large church , to a door that led down a staircase and into a basement . They walked through a maze of hallways and ended up at a room . It had a little bed , dresser and a lamp. The walls were empty except for a small window which showed the full moon outside . Rose motioned for her to go into the room , Diya did as asked . Rose left the room , shutting the door behind her . Diya exhausted from the day crawled into bed and fell asleep looking at the moon .

Diya was awoken by Rose the next morning . She had some food on a platter and some water . Diya ate quickly and changed into clothes Rose had picked out . She followed Rose through

The basement and back up the stairs . As they got close to the door , Diya could feel the excitement in the air . Rose opened the door and the church burst into life . Diya quickly grabbed a piece of Rose's dress as if it would keep her safe . Rose feeling her grab her dress looked down and smiled .

" It will be ok child " said Rose .

Diya followed Rose down the isle .

People were all around . Speaking in different words that she had never heard before . Before long Rose had found a seat and patted the seat beside her . Diya sat down and watched wide eyed all the action in front of her . A priest came out and spoke words unknown to the huge crowd of people , everyone sat down on cue and stopped talking . The priest went back to talking as the service had begun . Diya could feel someone looking at her , she turned to see a little girl her age ,the girl waved and smiled . Diya looked away quickly not sure of what to do . The service suddenly ended and the church erupted in chatter and movement once again. Diya looked for the little girl but she was gone.

Rose became like a mother to Diya . She was very strict but had a very loving nature to go with it . Diya followed Rose everyday and learned all the church duties . As Diya grew older she was assigned her own duties in the church .

Rose signed her up for school , as much as Diya argued going , Rose insisted that Diya be taught to be a lady .

Diya did not fit in well at school . She was dark , tall and thin while everyone else was of Caucasian descent . Diya lived in the church basement while everyone else had homes . Children would tease her , calling her a church mouse among other names . Some days she would hide in the bathroom to avoid any drama .

Diya wanted to quit because of the mean children but had fallen in love with the library and all the books . Everyday she would pick out a new adventure and read in the park by the church . Diya learned how to read quickly , she was top in all of her classes . Teachers loved her curiosity and willingness to learn .

One day after school , Diya made her way to her favorite reading spot . She heard yelling and then felt a sharp pain to her head . Looking around she saw a apple on the ground , rubbing her head she saw that one of the girls from her class had thrown it at her .

" Church mouse !! " yelled Shay , a girl from Diya's school . as she threw another apple at Diya . The other children laughed as she continued on .

" Parents did not want you church mouse " said Shay laughing .

From out of no where a blonde girl came running past Diya and straight to Shay , fists a swinging . She hit Shay right in the nose , blood flew everywhere . Everyone went silent and then Shay started screaming .

" Get out of here you bully !! "

yelled the blonde girl .

" Who are you ? " cried Shay holding her nose as blood poured out .

The blonde girl raised her fists and hit Shay again . Right in the jaw . Shay turned and ran , the other children following listening to her screams . The girl turned and walked up to Diya .

" Hi , I am Saphire " said the girl smiling .

" I am Diya " said Diya in surprise hoping the girl would not hit her as well . .

" So what are you doing ? " asked Saphire looking at the book in Diya's hands.

" Reading ? " answered Diya .

" Want to teach me ? " asked Saphire .

" To read ? " asked Diya surprised .

" Yes and I will keep those bullies away from you , deal ? " said Saphire sticking out her hand to shake .

" Deal " said Diya shaking her hand .

Everyday after school Diya would meet her new friend Saphire at their special spot . Saphire lived on the other side of town with her grandmother . They had no money to send her to school or barely take care of her . Saphire's parents had died when she was young , she was alone like Diya. Saphire would do odd jobs to help her grandmother , she would say that one day she would be so rich so that she would never have to work again . Diya would invite Saphire over but she refused to enter the church claiming she would burst into flames if she did .

As the months past, Saphire learned how to read and Diya was able to go to school without fear . They became good friends and trusted each other with all secrets . Diya loved her life and her friend . As life always does, it changed again for Diya that day .

" I have to go " said Saphire .

" Ok , see you tomorrow ? " said Diya packing up her book .

" No I have to leave town , I have to move Diya " said Saphire sadly .

" What are you talking about ? " said Diya surprised .

" My grandmother died . They are evicting me , I can't pay rent . I have to go " explained Saphire tears in her eyes .

" Where are you going ? " asked Diya now with tears in her eyes as well .

" My cousin lives a hour from here . She runs a tavern said I could work there and she would give me a place to live " explained Saphire .

" Come stay with me ! " exclaimed Diya hopefully .

" I can't ! I would start on fire remember ? " said Saphire with a sparkle in her eye .

" Right " said Diya sarcastically .

" We can always stay sisters if you want " said Saphire quietly .

" Yes " said Diya .

Saphire pulled out a pocket knife from her pocket and extended the blade . She sliced her finger across the top and it started bleeding .

" Your turn " said Saphire .

" For what " asked Diya staring at Saphire's finger bleeding .

" I cut both of our fingers and then we squeeze them together " explained Saphire .

" Why ? " asked Diya .

" Then we are blood sisters ! Forever ! " exclaimed Saphire smiling .

Diya held out her finger and closed her eyes waiting for the pain of the knife cutting her . It was fast and before she knew it she could feel Saphire's finger squeezing hers . Opening her eyes she saw Saphire smiling , Diya laughed and pulled her in for a hug .

" We are blood sisters !! " yelled Saphire to the sky laughing . She took Diya's hands and swung her round and round .

" Always and forever ? " said Diya.

33

" Always and forever !! " said
Saphire suddenly serious .

Diya pulled out her favorite book .
It was a tale of two friends .

" Here , take this with you " said
Diya .

" I can't take your favorite book !! "
exclaimed Saphire in surprise .

" Yes you can ! Keep up on your
reading and don't forget about me ! " said Diya
warmly hoping Saphire would never forget about
her . Saphire took the book and placed it carefully
in her bag .

" Thank you sister " said Saphire .

They hugged and said goodbye and
went their separate ways . Loneliness grabbed
Diya's hand as she walked back to the church
knowing she would not be seeing Saphire for a long
time to come .

Chapter 4

Diya graduated with honors . Rose
beamed with joy and would tell her over and over
how proud she was . Now that Diya had
graduated , she could take over a full time position
at the church . Diya loved the church and swore to
devote her life to God . She spent Sunday mornings
with the church children teaching them how to
read from the bible . Diya would do crafts and loved
telling stories . Rose and other clergy would praise
Diya and her skills , claiming she was a prodigy of
the church . Diya started a library in the church ,
full of hymn and prayer books . It was the first of
its kind and to be run by a woman was unheard
of in all of the land . Diya also started a bible group
where other church members could come and

read the bible and find meaning . Almost a debate place at times , it became a weekly thing and drew in members from all around .

On one lively night , a discussion was going strong and there were several new faces in the debate .

" Christ was human , therefore his human and divine natures are equally important ! " exclaimed a young man with zest . The older men in the group murmured in disagreement .

Diya's ears perked up , it was usually the older church members who had any discussions that sometimes got heated . She looked around the room and saw who was causing the uproar . It was a young man who looked her age , he was tall , blond and green eyes . Very handsome Diya thought to herself . He looked like he was having a fun time upsetting the elders in the room .

" Christ is divine and that is his only nature " responded one of the older men.

" But he was human was he not ? "
responded the young man quickly with a smile .

" Blasphemy ! " said one of the
older men angerly .

" Now gentlemen , calm down . We
are all entitled to our opinion " said Diya trying to
calm down the room . She could feel the anger
rising . The group picked up their bibles and
started shuffling around getting ready to leave .

" Thank you Diya " said one of the
older church members before leaving .

" Yes , thank you . Is it Diya ? That
is a beautiful name . I am Mica " said the young
man

" Thank you and yes I am Diya .
Mica is a unusual name ? " said Diya blushing
and finding it hard to speak . What was the matter
with her ? She cleared her throat .

" My name is Micheal but I shorted
it to Mica " explained Mica smiling .

" Great job Diya . I love our weekly

Bible studies . Keeps our minds fresh . Right ? "
said another church member as they passed by
Diya leaving . Diya nodded and looked back at
Mica . He was gathering his things .

" See you around " said Mica as he
stepped around people and headed out the door .

" He is a nice gentleman "
whispered Rose into Diya's ear .

" Where did you come from ? " said
Diya surprised .

" I am always around my dear "
said Rose .

" That you are " replied Diya .

" What about that man ? He seems
nice and handsome " said Rose smiling .

" I have no idea , I just met him "
answered Diya annoyed .

Rose had been mentioning marriage
daily since Diya had graduated . She said it was
time to get married and have some children . Diya
was not sure marriage was for her as she enjoyed

her church work so much . Marriage would be a fulltime job and ad many duties to her already full list . Rose reminded her daily that she was not getting any younger and did not want Diya to spend her life as a spinster .

Mica showed back up the next day with flowers in hand . He showed up everyday there after as well , always with a smile and some sort of interesting gift . He would praise Diya for what a strong woman she was and how he admired her .

They soon became a official couple . The church was in full support of their budding relationship . Diya and Mica were soon obsessed with each other and together from dawn till dusk . Diya loved everything about Mica and was surprised at how quickly he took over her heart and mind .

Diya still took her time everyday to go to the park by the church . She would sit and read listening to the forest , or she would sit lost in thought thinking about her lost friends the Floras.

Diya had tried closing her eyes and leaving bread , tried whistling and even tried calling out at times . No Flora would ever show up . As time went on , Diya often wondered if she had made them up in her childhood mind . They had seemed so real though .

Her mind would wander to Saphire as well . Diya had sent messages to the tavern that Saphire had spoken of but they were all returned . Looking at her finger she could barely see any evidence that it had ever been cut at all .

Diya would pray for the Floras and Saphire , hoping they would all find each other again one day . They were her family , she felt complete with them . Which made her think of Mica . He was such a sweet man and was so full of possibilities . He had a mind of his own but was still very kind and humble . Mica came from a good family who had already promised him a house once he married . As if on cue Mica appeared and sat down beside her .

" I was looking for you " whispered Mica sweetly in Diya's ear .

" Well you have found me " whispered Diya back .

" Can I keep you forever ? " whispered Mica running his lips across her neck .

Diya gasped and pulled away .

" What is forever ? Is it now ? Is it later ? Is your forever until next week or until the end of time ? " asked Diya playfully .

" Sweet maiden my forever is until the end of time under our gods eyes and longer then that " answered Mica promptly .

" Is that a lie you tell me or yourself ? " said Diya .

" Oh you are extra cheeky today " said Mica laughing as her grabbed Diya's hand to hold .

Diya turned her head to gaze at the trees tops . The clouds were big and grand threatening a storm with its wind .

" I have been thinking a lot lately Diya . The world is changing . We are not getting any younger " said Mica thoughtfully .

" What are you saying ? That I am old ? " said Diya laughing .

" No of course not " said Mica all flustered .

Diya wondered why he was acting so weird and had searched her out in the first place .

" I need a wife Diya " said Mica suddenly .

" So you want me to find you one ? " asked Diya in a teasing way .

" No ! Oh gosh I am just saying everything wrong " said Mica looking down at the ground sadly .

Diya squeezed Mica's hand . She had never seen him so flustered before . Mica got up from the bench and then got down on one knee , he grabbed Diya's hand .

" Diya , will you marry me ? " asked Mica looking into Diya's eyes .

Diya was speechless for a minute .

She stared into Mica's eyes looking for the answer .

Diya silently prayed for a sign if she was to marry Mica . She had asked for signs from god before but nothing had ever happened . This time she looked up and a single feather was floating high up in the air , above her head , swirling and dropping towards her . Diya watched in amazement as the feather dropped on her lap . Mica reached over and picked up the feather and held it for her to see .

" Well ? " asked Mica softly .

" Yes " answered Diya staring at the feather .

" Yes ? " said Mica with excitement .

Diya nodded yes and Mica jumped up and screamed in joy . Diya stood up and they hugged tightly .

" You have made me so happy , lets make it official " said Mica as he dug in his pocket .

Mica pulled his hand out of his pocket and grabbed Diya's left hand , he gently placed a ring on it . She looked down and her eyes filled with tears . It was the prettiest ring she had ever seen and it fit her perfectly . It was a gold band with a diamond set upon it . The diamond sparkled no matter which way the light hit it .

" It was my mothers " said Mica .

" It is beautiful " said Diya .

" Not as beautiful as you are , my wife to be " said Mica smiling .

Chapter 5

The church was a buzz . Rose was over the moon . Diya was getting married and it turned out to be sooner then later . Mica had insisted that they get married right away . His mother already unhappy he was marrying Diya , who she referred to as a church orphan , was extremely upset at the short time frame . Mica wanted the wedding in two weeks and Diya agreed . He said why waste anymore time when it seemed war was breaking out across the world.

With everyday that got closer Diya grew more and more excited at the thought of living in her own house and being a wife , perhaps one day a mother . One morning she awoke and found a white long flowing wedding dress hanging in her room . It had little beads that looked like diamonds , hundreds of them all sewed into the dress , which gave it a shimmering effect . Diya quickly tried it on , it fit her perfectly . It had a high neckline and fit tight until her hips and then it flared out . She spung in the room giving the dress life .

" Do you like it ? " asked Rose suddenly stepping into the room .

" Do I like it ? I LOVE it ! " exclaimed Diya smiling .

" You look so beautiful " said Rose .

" Where did you find this ? It is simply amazing " said Diya gushing with happiness .

" I made it " said Rose proudly .

" Seriously ? " said Diya surprised .

" Yes , seriously " replied Rose with a hint of sarcasm .

Diya ran across the room and wrapped her arms around Rose hugging her as tight as she could .

" Thank you so much " said Diya
not sure if she should laugh or cry .

" You came here nothing but a little
shadow of a girl and now look at you Diya . I would
only be so proud to call you my daughter at this
moment " said Rose warmly .

" You are my mother as far as I am
concerned " said Diya seriously .

" Thank you " said Rose tearing up .

" Now lets get ready for the wedding
of the century ! " exclaimed Diya as she swirled
around her room in her glimmering dress .

A week went by so fast . Diya had
never felt so much pressure before . She had to
pick out a cake , wedding colors , what food and
write vows . Mica had invited her for a day trip
away from the church , last day as boyfriend and
girlfriend he said . Although Diya was stressed out
with everything that had to be done she was excited
to get out of the church and explore somewhere

new.

"My love" yelled Mica from the stairs to the basement of the church.

"Coming !!" yelled Diya back as she weaved her way from her room to the stairs.

Diya made her way to the stairs and greeted Mica with a kiss on his cheek. They proceeded out of the church holding hands. Mica rushed over and opened the door for Diya, once outside she could see a huge carriage waiting. She turned to go back into the church.

"Where are you going?" asked Mica.

"The carriage. It must be for the pastor, I will go and let him know" answered Diya.

"Diya, that is for us" said Mica.

The driver of the carriage got down and opened the little door.

"Come" said Mica grabbing Diya's hand and leading her to the carriage.

Diya jumped up into the carriage ,
it was covered with velvet and gems , she was
afraid to sit down on the cushions as they looked
brand new .

" Sit down , its ok " said Mica as if
he could read her mind .

" This is so nice Mica " said Diya .

" You deserve it " said Mica .

The carriage took off with a jolt and
then settled down to a steady pace . Diya sat
frozen and wide eyed .

" Have you ever been a carriage
before " asked Mica .

" No " answered Diya .

" It takes a minute to get used to , it
is much faster then walking to where I want to
take you " said Mica .

" Where are we going ? You never
told me " said Diya relaxing a little .

" Porticus of Pompey " answered
Mica .

" What is that ? " asked Diya .

" A public park , it is beautiful . It has big trees , flowers , fountains and a huge theater . I think you will like it . I have lunch packed for us " answered Mica .

" It sounds very nice " said Diya as she gazed out the carriage window .

" Your very nice " said Mica moving closer to Diya .

" Your in a great mood today " said Diya .

" I am marrying the woman of my dreams next week , how could I not be happy ? " exclaimed Mica .

They kissed and sat in silence for the remainder of the trip .

Within a hour they pulled up to the most beautiful park Diya had ever seen . She went to open the door but Mica motioned not to . Soon enough the door was opened by the carriage driver , he held out his hand for Diya .

" This is amazing Mica " said Diya gushing with excitement . The park was as promised with a huge fountain and trees . The flowers were perfectly organized and the grass was all short like it had been just cut .

" Let's walk " said Mica grabbing the basket with their lunch .

They walked around the park and eventually found a spot by a huge open stage area . It was busy with street vendors trying to sell their wares . The park was full with people as it was one of the warmest days in awhile . Mica quickly emptied the basket and set up for lunch . Diya joined him on the ground still amazed with all the action and the scenery .

" Here , eat sweetheart . We have lots of time to look around " said Mica handing Diya a biscuit and some cheese .

Diya gladly took the biscuit and started eating , she watched the vendors with curiosity .

" What has your attention ? " asked
Mica .

" The pentagram over there on that
vendors cart " answered Diya .

" Yes I see that . Just ignore it "
said Mica with a frown .

Diya finished her food and cleaned
up the lunch putting it all back in the basket . She
got up and brushed herself off .

" Where are you going ? " asked
Mica .

" I just want to look " said Diya .

" It is the devils work " said Mica .

" Yes and I want to see who hangs it
in pride ? I am just curious . Don't worry , I am on
gods side silly " explained Diya as she started
walking to the pentagram .

" DIYA ! " yelled Mica .

Diya heard Mica yell but ignored
him and kept walking towards the pentagram . She
was not some dog to be told what to do .

As Diya got closer she heard a lady ask the people at the table if they would like a reading of their futures for a small donation . Diya was shocked . Right here so close to home the devil was at work ? The people declined and started to walk away , Diya stepped in front of the table and went to speak but then stopped . She stood speechless .

" Diya !! " exclaimed Saphire in surprise .

There was Saphire , all dressed in black with blonde hair glowing , she was sitting at a table with a deck of cards in her hands . The cards did not look like playing cards , they had different pictures on them . Diya watched Saphire shuffle the cards and then lay them out one by one.

" What are you doing here ? What happened to the tavern ? Are you ok ? " asked Diya in disbelief .

" That didn't work out for me . You look good Diya , I have missed you " said Saphire .

" I have missed you as well . What is all of this ? " said Diya motioning to the table , cards and pentagram .

" I needed money and it turns out I am good with the cards , I like it , I am going to be famous one day . What are you doing ? Who is that guy over there that yelled at you ? " asked Saphire looking over to Mica who was starting to walk over .

" I am getting married next week " said Diya awkwardly .

" To him ? " said Saphire giggling .

Diya nodded .

" So your marrying for money eh ? " said Saphire sarcastically .

" No ! " said Diya defensively .

Mica walked up and put his arm around Diya .

" Are you alright ? " asked Mica looking at Saphire with distaste .

" I am fine Mica " answered Diya laughing .

" Shall we ? " said Mica confused at Diya's laughter .

Diya looked at Mica and then to Saphire .

" Yes " answered Diya grabbing Mica's hand as she started walking away .

" Madam , your reading ? " asked Saphire pointing to the cards laid out on the table .

Diya stopped to look at Saphire . She wanted to run and hug her .

" Your world will soon change , but not the way you think it will " said Saphire quietly .

" Goodbye " said Diya .

Diya and Mica walked away at a fast pace .

" Do you know her ? " asked Mica looking at Diya with concern .

" I thought she was someone I used to know " said Diya sadly .

" Well she is right , your world is going to change soon " said Mica .

Chapter 6

It was 3 days before the wedding .
The church was full of friends , clergy and Mica's
family . It was rehearsal night with a formal dinner
to follow . Diya sat quietly in the corner watching
all the action .

" Are you alright little bird ? " asked
Rose as she appeared out of no where .

" Yes .. Gosh you are quiet . You
scared me " said Diya laughing .

" You were lost in another world it
looked like " said Rose .

" Yes I guess I was " said Diya .

Cheers broke out and Mica laughed
loudly . He pointed over to Diya and then blew her
kisses . Diya winked and pretended to catch the

Kisses from out of the air . Mica winked back at Diya and went back to his lively conversation .

" It will be empty without you here " said Rose .

" I can stay " said Diya quickly .

" I think it is to late for that " said Rose pointing towards Mica .

" I agree " said Diya smiling .

" What are your plans ? " asked Rose .

" I am thinking some babies " whispered Diya .

" What ! " exclaimed Rose with a huge smile .

" Shhhh ! " whispered Diya laughing .

" I can not wait " said Rose with excitement in her voice.

" Rose , can I ask you something ? " asked Diya with a serious voice .

" Yes child " said Rose .

" Why was I brought here ? " asked Diya . It haunted her everyday not knowing .

" I don't know " answered Rose looking away from Diya .

" Did my mother sell me ? " asked Diya .

" No and well yes " said Rose .

Diya looked at Rose perplexed .

" She was not your mother . Story has it that she found you wandering in the fields one day . She decided to keep you as her own and then one day Rion showed up , told her to give you to him , you did not belong to her and gave her money for any trouble . At least that is what I have heard . I am sorry child " explained Rose .

" Who sent Rion ? " asked Diya . She was shocked with all this new information .

" I don't know " answered Rose .

" Well you must know why I was brought here ? " asked Diya looking around the room at the clergy members curiously wondering

If perhaps it was one of them .

" I don't know that either Diya . You showed up one day and I was told to make room for you . Paster Mike had said he had already made arrangements for you to stay as a orphan . " said Rose .

" Who is Pastor Mike ? " asked Diya . She had never heard of a Pastor Mike at anytime growing up in the church .

" He passed away within the first year you were here " said Rose .

Cheers erupted again echoing throughout the church . A bell was rung and dinner was announced . The crowd cheered and people started towards the hall .

" So you don't know anything else that could help me figure this out ? " asked Diya perplexed .

Rose looked around the room as if someone might hear her .

" I have something for you , it might

Help . Come with me " said Rose .

Rose headed for the front of the church . It was empty now with everyone gone for supper . She picked up a small statue of the lord and pulled a coiled piece of paper out from the bottom of it . Rose quickly put it in Diya's hand .

" It is all I have to help you " whispered Rose .

" Ladies " said Mica from the other end of the church .

" We are coming " said Diya in a cheery voice as she looked at Rose .

" Thank you " whispered Diya as they walked to dinner .

Diya could feel the coiled up piece of paper in her pocket all throughout dinner . She wondered what it could possibly say on it . Diya hoped it was a name , perhaps a family member . She had hoped that Rose had more information then she had . Diya had spent years trying to be brave enough to ask Rose and now she was disappointed with her answers . Maybe she was nothing more then a lost orphan that the church took pity on . Diya felt the paper and had hope that it held all the answers to her questions .

"Tonight was a success " whispered Mica into Diya's ear . She jumped in surprise .

"Yes " said Diya .

"You seem off tonight " said Mica looking closely at Diya as if she were sick . He felt her forehead and then kissed it .

"No I am fine . Just a lot on my mind " answered Diya .

"To late to change your mind , just so you know " said Mica sweetly .

"You are not getting rid of me that easily " said Diya smiling . It was true . She adored Mica and could not wait to be his wife . Diya knew how lucky she was .

"I love you " said Mica .

"And I love you " said Diya .

"Three more days " said Mica .

" Till forever " said Diya smiling .

" Always and forever " said Mica.

It was a perfect night Diya thought to herself as she watched the last of the clergy leave the church . She quickly cleaned up and headed to her little library of books . Diya was excited to see what was on the mystery piece of paper . Sitting down on her favorite chair she carefully pulled the paper out of her pocket and examined it . Diya slowly unrolled the paper and found it had two names on it .

Di lux

That was the only thing on the paper . Was it her mothers name ?

Diya had never heard of any of these names before . She decided she would ask some elders in the morning if they knew where the name was from or better yet , who it is . Diya got up and headed down to her bedroom . She found herself going slowly as if to record every memory of the church . In three days she would be moving

In with Mica . His family had bought them a house about 20 minutes away . Diya knew she was still close but the church had been her only home for as long as she could remember .

" Di lux " said Diya to her empty room as she entered it .

Diya undressed and got into bed . Looking up at her window she could see the moon as full as the first night she had arrived .

Diya tossed and turned all night . She dreamt of being a child and playing with the Floras , then she was lost in a forest calling out for them but it was so dark . Diya kept smelling smoke and hearing screams . She saw herself as a child , crying , lost in a field . Then the woman she thought was her mother pick her up . The children from school chasing her through a maze . No matter how much Diya tried she could not wake up . More smoke , so much smoke she could not see anything at all . Then Diya was on a beach , sand all around , she could feel the heat on her

skin . The sun was so bright Diya could barely
see . Her eyes adjusted and she could see the ocean
in front of her , there was a boat . As it got closer
she could see someone standing on the boat . They
were screaming and waving their hands in the air .

      " What ? " yelled Diya to the
stranger on the boat .

      The boat came closer .

      " WAKE UP " yelled the stranger.

Chapter 7

Diya woke up unable to breathe .
She started gasping for air . Her blanket was heavy
as if it was being held down . Opening her eyes she
could see that she was laying in a pile of chaos .
Pieces of wood among other things were scattered
all over her . Her bedroom ceiling once old , grey
and made of brick was now gone . Diya could now
see the sky way up above. The smell of smoke was
thick in the air , Diya realized she was completely
covered in a thick layer of ash . She tried to move
but had barely any strength . Diya started
screaming and then went unconscious .

This time waking up was different ,
the air smelt fresh and it was easier to breathe .
Diya opened her eyes and to her surprise she was

In a clean bed in a huge white room . She sat up and swung her legs over the bed , it took a minute before Diya stood up and then came crashing back down on the bed . The door to the room opened and a lady dressed in a white cloak came in .

" Hello , I am Jackie . How are you feeling ? " asked the lady .

" What happened ? " whispered Diya , her throat was so sore she could barely talk .

" There was a huge fire , burnt down the church and everyone in it , well , except you " explained Jackie .

Diya went to talk but started coughing .

" You have inhaled a lot of smoke , take your time . You will be coughing it all up the next couple days " said Jackie .

Diya nodded and motioned to the water on the night table . Jackie handed it to her watching Diya gulp down the water .

" Do you remember anything ? It is

66

A miracle you are alive " said Jackie .

" No I don't " answered Diya . Her mind was reeling trying to grasp what had just happened .

" I know it is none of my business , but how did you get all those beautiful marks ? " asked Jackie looking at Diya's arms .

Diya looked down at her arms and gasped , they both were covered In black artwork . As she examined herself she realized the markings started at her feet and ran right up to her neck . Some markings looked like vines while others were pictures of animals and other abstract art .

" What did you do to me ? " asked Diya with tears on her eyes looking at the lady .

" I did not do anything . When we washed the ash off they were there . I swear " said Jackie with wide eyes .

" Where am I ? " asked Diya suddenly . Where was Mica and Rose ?

" You are at a Euros Convent for

young nuns in training " explained Jackie .

" Where is my fiance ? " asked
Diya .

Jackie's smile turned into a frown
and she looked down at the floor .

" Is he ok ? " asked Diya suddenly
worried .

" Oh he is fine " answered Jackie
still not making eye contact with Diya .

" Well then where is he ? " asked
Diya impatiently .

" He is not coming " said Jackie
quietly .

" Why ? " asked Diya .

" Well the church says you are a
abomination " blurted out Jackie .

" Abomination ? " said Diya
shocked .

" Many people died in the fire yet
here you are not even a scratch or burn mark , and
you say those marks on your body are new ? The

church has deemed you a abomination , the devils

work " explained Jackie as she cautiously looked at

Diya .

" That is not true ! " exclaimed Diya

surprised . Diya stood back up and started walking

to the door .

" Where are you going ? " asked

Jackie .

" This is a sick joke . I am going to

my fiance " said Diya as she walked out of the

room . She found her way out of the convent and

stood for a minute taking in the fresh air and

sunshine . Diya started down the road towards the

church . As Diya got closer to the church she

noticed people stopping and staring at her . She

thought at first she was being paranoid until

someone yelled Devils spawn . Diya stopped in her

tracks and turned around . It was her friend Ally

who ran the bread shop down the road .

" What did you say ?" asked Diya .

" BEGONE WITCH " yelled Ally .

Diya's jaw dropped . She had never seen Ally mad .

" I am not a witch ! " exclaimed Diya .

" WITCH ! WITCH ! " yelled Ally .

Neighbours started to gather around Ally joining in on the chant .

" WITCH ! " the crowd yelled .

Someone threw a egg , it hit Diya in the shoulder and broke . Diya screamed in surprise and started to run away from the crowd .Diya ran until she was out of breath , as she turned the corner she stopped and fell to her knees . Where her church used to stand was a huge black hole . There was nothing left . It was all gone . Diya rubbed her eyes in disbelief . No matter what she did , the picture in front of her never changed . Her home since a child , her library , all gone . Diya regained herself and got up from the ground , brushing the egg off her shoulder . She started towards Mica's , she knew he would

understand and help her . Within twenty minutes
she arrived at Mica's house , well it was their house
to be , as soon as they were married . Diya quickly
patted down her hair and knocked on the front
door . She could hear shuffling and voices inside
yet no one would answer . She knocked again , this
time much louder and waited . Finally she heard
footsteps coming to the front door and watched the
handle turn to open .

Mica pulled open the door and
stood back with a look of surprise on his face .

" Mica ! " said Diya smiling , she
was happy to see him .

" Hello " said Mica quietly , he stood
unmoving from the entrance .

" Are you going to invite me in ?
Why did you not come to see me ? " asked Diya
confused .

" I can't Diya " said Mica looking
away from her .

" Why ? " asked Diya still confused.

" Your ... " said Mica unable to
finish his sentence as he broke into tears . Diya
went to hug him but he stepped back with a look of
fear on his face .

" I am what ? " said Diya .

" You should not be alive " said
Mica suddenly .

" But I am alive Mica . It is a
miracle " said Diya .

" Is it a miracle or is it the devils
work ? " said Mica bravely as he stared at the
markings on her arm .

" I cant believe this ! First I lose the
only home I have and now you are telling me I am
the devils work ? This is ludicrous Mica ! "
exclaimed Diya with hurt in her voice .

Mica looked away , Diya could see a
tear fall down his cheek and onto the ground . They
stood in silence .

" Mica ? " whispered Diya .

" You have to go " said Mica .

72

" Go ? Where ? " said Diya in a panic . Her head was spinning . She had no were to go . The church and Mica were her home .

" Where is Rose ? " asked Diya in hope . Rose would know what to do . She would believe Diya .

" She is dead Diya " said Mica .

" No ! " whimpered Diya in shock .

" She went in to look for you when the fire started Diya , Rose never came back out " said Mica sadly .

Diya let out a scream . It was one of loss , hurt and pain . She could not believe this was happening . Mica stood wide eyed and offered no comfort .

" Please go now " said Mica with no emotion .

" Please Mica . I have no where to go . I thought you loved me " pleaded Diya .

" I loved you , I have no idea who or what you are now " said Mica as he backed up and

73

shut his front door . Diya could hear him set the lock .

" You son of a BITCH ! " yelled Diya in anger . She bent over and picked up some rocks and threw them at the house . She could see him peeking out of his bedroom window .

" I CURSE YOU ! " yelled Diya angerly as she walked away . She had no idea how to curse someone but was so angry she wanted to scare Mica .

Chapter 8

The next couple weeks were the worst weeks of Diya's life . She had always been treated very well with the church, now everyone she met treated her like garbage . It was shocking and humbling at the same time . Not one person from the church would give her one minute of time , either calling her a witch , devils spawn or just straight out ignoring her . Diya starving of hunger would wait outside in the alleyways of the restaurant's for scraps . She slept in the trees with a old blanket the nuns had given her . The nuns were the only people who would acknowledge her existence , but even then they would always keep Diya at a arms distance and stare as if she would hurt them at any given time . The marks on her body would not go away . She had tried scrubbing them off while bathing in a nearby creek , but all it did was leave her skin red and swollen . Diya did not want to live another day , she was consumed by grief . She did not understand why her god would betray her like this ? Lead all these people into believing lies ?

Diya walked to a nearby bridge , looking down at the moving water she knew if she jumped now , she could end all of her misery . Diya stood on the edge of the walkway , the wind blowing so hard against her as if it was trying to stop her from jumping , it caressed her like a gentle giant .

" God ! I don't know why you have forsaken me ! I am your loyal and humble servant ! I pray you let me in heavens gate when I arrive " yelled Diya into the night sky as she closed her eyes and jumped off the bridge .

Diya felt as of she weighed nothing and then hit the water as if it was a brick wall .

Diya could feel her bones shatter as she hit the water . The current picked her up as shot her down the river as if she was a ball to be thrown . She felt her lungs slowly fill with water , her body in so much pain she eagerly accepted the water into her lungs to end the misery . The last thing Diya saw was a single star in the night sky shining so bright and then everything went dark .

A bird was singing a sweet song when Diya awoke . She was laying on the shoreline of the river , trying to move Diya puked up a bunch of water . Looking around she did not recognize any of the surroundings and wondered how far the river had carried her . She was amazed that she was still alive as she was sure she had died .

This started a obsession within Diya . She spent the next twenty years trying to kill herself and not succeeding .

She had tried poisoning herself , a painful and horrible way that lasted weeks before finally letting her die .

Diya had stabbed herself , another horrible death . She watched herself bleed out convinced she had found the way as she passed out only to awake the next day fine but with bloody clothes . Snake bites , hanging , gun shots , beatings , jumping from the highest cliffs she could find , crushing her skull . Diya could not kill herself no matter how hard she tried . She would always awake the next day , all parts that had been broken , now fixed . As the years went by she questioned if she was indeed cursed or of devils blood .

Not only was she unable to die , Diya noticed as the years went by she was not aging . Not one wrinkle , not one blemish , she looked exactly the same everyday .

" I give up !! What do you want from me ? " screamed Diya at the sky as if she was speaking directly to god . Silence . Diya wondered what she had done to anger god . She must have angered him for her to be in this hell .

Diya walked for weeks deep into the forest . She walked until she could no longer walk , stopping beside a small creek she decided that this was it . Her new home . She was tired of hiding . Tired of trying to end her life . Diya was going to live .

Picking up stones from all around , Diya built a stone house . It took years but she had nothing but time on her side . Diya did not stop at the house , a garden was planted from seeds she gathered from all around , a fence was built to protect the garden from wandering deer . She found more stones and built a chapel so she could pray to god . Diya wanted god to see what a faithful servant she was . A creek ran past her house all year long , Diya dug out a hole and lined it with rocks then made a trench from the creek into the hole , she made her own bathing spot . The years went by fast, Diya made her home everything she could of dream of and more . It became her sanctuary , her home and most of all

It kept her mind busy . Diya's mind was her worst enemy , if she distracted her mind with a million projects maybe she could forget all her pain .

A swing was built , high up in the trees . Diya broke her neck twice building it , falling from the tree onto the ground , waking the next day good as new . It was worth it , she would climb up to the swing every evening , to watch the sunset and gaze at the stars. Mostly she just wanted to feel closer to god on her swing , as if he would be able to hear her prayers and pleas easier.

Diya could not provide everything she needed to survive and stay somewhat sane As the years went by she made a map of all villages or settlements near by , she found she could trade furs for what she needed . It reminded her of when she was with the woman she called her mother and their trips to the little village . War had broken out across Europe , it was hard times for all . Diya would trade for salt , sugar and books , among other little things she would need .

It took over 50 years before Diya returned to where the church had been . They had long ago cleaned it up and a brand new building sat in its place . She had inquired about Mica and his family to learn that things had not worked out so well for them . Diya tried not to smile at the new information but thought it was funny how life worked out . Apparently it was her fault , she had cursed Mica and his family and disappeared into the night . Within weeks Mica became so sick that he had to use a wheel chair , he died only a year later . His family went broke and were ran out of the town . Diya had heard a word called karma , where life always evens out , what's goes around comes around . She was starting to believe in karma .

Diya would inquire about Saphire on her trips away from home but no one knew who she was talking about . Eventually she quit asking as she knew that Saphire would be very old and possibly dead by now .

Diya could remember everything ,
except for the name on the piece of paper . She
would try and try but it seemed as if it had never
happened . She could recall getting the piece of
paper from Rose and opening it . But the paper was
always blank in her head . The only clue she had
to her life was lost in her mind somewhere and
refused to come back out .

Time had slipped by without notice,
one day turning into the next. Diya had made
friends with a little fox she had found as a young
baby . Somehow it was alone , so she tucked it up
and cared for it . The fox who she named Foxy grew
and was always by her side . Then one day she
looked at her fox friend and realized that he had
grown old and would soon pass on . Diya cried so
hard when her foxy died . How life could be so
unfair . She was alone yet again . Devasted Diya
climbed up to her swing on that rainy day , she did
not even make it before slipping and falling to her
death.

This time when she awoke , it was different . The sun was peeking through the leaves onto her . She took a huge breath of air and opened her eyes . The sky above her was all full of tiny sparkles . Diya closed her eyes and opened them again thinking something must be wrong with her eyes . But the sparkles were still there , falling like tiny drops off rain . Then she saw the feather . Floating down towards her , as it had before in the past . Swirling and spinning on its own journey to Diya . She lay on the ground motionless watching the sparkles and the feather fall towards her . Maybe this was death she wondered . The feather fell onto her chest reaching its destination . The falling sparkles fading and then gone , just a memory in the wind .

Diya took another breath of air and sat up , grabbing the feather in her hand . Then she heard a whistle . A familiar whistle . One she had not herd since a child . She quickly got to her feet and whistled back , she turned in circles trying to find which direction the whistle was coming from . Again she heard it , this time above her . Looking up she could see a Flora , sitting on her swing

Chapter 9

Diya stood speechless watching the Flora . It turned and jumped off of the swing flying down to her , Stopping right in front of her face .

" Hello Diya " said the Flora .

" Hello " said Diya wondering just how hard she had hit her head when she had hit the ground .

" We have been looking a long time for you " said the Flora .

A long time was right . Diya estimated that she was hundreds of years old now , she had lost count a long time ago . What was the point when she never really aged . She had long ago given up thinking about the Flora's , chalking up her memories to child hood fantasy .

But here floating in front of her was a Flora .

" Hello " said Diya repeating herself not sure of what to say .

" Do you remember me ? " asked the Flora .

" Yes . How are you talking ? " asked Diya . She did not remember the Flora's doing anything other then copying her when she spoke as a child ,

" We learned while looking for you " answered the Flora as it flew around Diya .

" Why were you looking for me ? " asked Diya now curious .

" We missed you " answered the Flora .

" I missed you to . Are you the same Flora ?" asked Diya now full of questions .

" I am the same Flora " answered the Flora proudly . It puffed its little chest out in pride .

" What is your name ?" asked Diya.

" I am Flora " answered the Flora proudly .

" Flora " said Diya trying not to laugh .

Flora nodded its little head in agreement when Diya said its name .

" Are you the only one ? " asked Diya looking around .

" No " answered Flora .

Diya looked at the Flora and happiness spread across her heart . Her long lost friends were still alive and well .

What a great day .

The Flora suddenly gave a long whistle , so loud it was unexpected from such a tiny little creature . It surprised Diya and made her jump . Hundreds of Floras came flying from above and all around Diya suddenly . Diya gave a loud cheer to all the Floras , mostly out of shock and surprise , then started smiling . They were mostly all white and identical in size .

Diya watched in amazement .

" Shhhh " whispered Diya suddenly . She watched all the Flora's land on the tree branches at once . They paused as if waiting for her next command . Diya laughed out loud .

" Go ! " yelled Diya .

The Floras instantly flew up in the air in a fancy swirl and disappeared . Diya frowned at first but realized she did tell them to go . She put her lips together and tried to mimic the Floras long whistle and to her joy the Floras came back and resumed playing and flying around .

" Are you kidding me ? " whispered Diya to herself .

" What is kidding ? " asked Flora still hovering in the same place watching Diya .

" Are they listening to me ? " asked Diya in shock .

" Yes . You are ... like us " answered Flora..

" Like you ? " asked Diya .

" Yes " said Flora .

Diya went back to watching the

Floras play .

From that day forward everywhere

Diya went the Floras followed . She enjoyed the

attention and what little bit of conversation they

had . Flora was the best speaker of them and the

most knowledgeable of the Floras .

Diya started training the Floras

everyday . Voice and hand commands . They were

amazing and soon she would barely motion and

they would already do her bidding . She felt blessed

to have them at her will , although she was not

sure to what purpose . She questioned Edward to

no end and it answered promptly and patiently to

every question . She found out that the Floras were

indeed like her in many ways . They had just

showed up one day (as Diya had just shown up in

the field as a child), they never aged and they

could not die . They had tried talking to other

people throughout time , people had always tried

to put them in cage's . Floras were not pets Flora said with distaste .

" Are you good or bad ? " asked Diya one day while she was swinging on her swing in the trees .

" We just are " answered Flora sitting next to Diya on the swing .

" You just are what ? " asked Diya .

" We not good or bad , we just are . What is the word ? We just exist . Go where we want , when we want . Like you " answered Flora .

That day Diya changed a little . She no longer felt alone in the world . She was simply existing the same as the Floras . Not good not bad just simply Diya . It was a perfect day .

And they did exist , together , in the forest , in Diya's little paradise for hundreds of years . The Floras became almost like a second hand to Diya , seeming to read her thoughts instantly . She could not remember a time before the Floras .

As time went by the villages became bigger and more people ventured out into the forested areas wanting to have their own land . Diya could watch the progress decade by decade on her swing . The Floras would go and spy on neighbours and report back to Diya . She worried they would have to leave their enchanted home one day . That day came sooner then later to Diya's dismay .

" Hello !! " yelled a mans voice .

Diya stopped in her tracks , the Floras disappeared . Did she just hear someone ?

" HELLO ? " yelled another mans voice .

Diya walked slowly to her house and could see two men standing beside it .

" Hello ? Can I help you with something ? " asked Diya bravely .

" Well hello " said a tall , dark bearded man as he looked Diya up and down .

" I was not expecting her to walk out of the forest " said the second man licking his lips . He was a short , chubby little man .

" Where's your husband ? " asked the first man looking around .

" He will be right back " said Diya lying . These men did not look like nice guys . She looked around for anything she could use as a weapon and could see nothing . Panic set in and her heart started beating faster .

" So your alone ? " asked the first man not moving his eyes off of Diya .

" No " said Diya firmly .

" That sounds like a yes " said the second man with a laugh .

The two men started walking towards Diya .

" Back off !! " exclaimed Diya .

They both started laughing and continued walking towards her . The shorter one started undoing his buckle on his pants .

Diya screamed and closed her eyes wishing they would go away . She felt the wind blow her hair as if she in a tornado , then heard the men start to scream . Opening her eyes she watched the Floras in formation circle the men closer and closer until they picked apart the men piece by piece . Once done they flew tight in a tunnel up to the heavens until Diya could not see them anymore . She looked to where the two men had been standing and now there was 2 bloody piles of what was bones and skin . Once realizing what the piles were , Diya started to puke .

The remainder of the day Diya was in shock . She had no idea her furry little friends could be cold blooded killers . She also was not ready to be found by the world , which meant it was time to leave. Diya knew this day was coming as she had been lucky enough to spend over a thousand years living in the same place . She knew now that the Floras would always be with her , no matter where she went .

Diya barely slept that night . She worried about what her and the Floras future may hold . Her dreams were all scattered images of the church , Mica and the coiled up piece of paper . Diya tossed and turned trying to wake up and then Rose was there . She walked over and hugged Diya warmly and whispered in her ear " Time to go " . Rose sat up in her bed in a sweat .

Chapter 9

Diya spent months traveling around the region looking for a purpose or reason . She felt lost , unsure and depressed . Diya was again begging for food and sleeping under neath any safe cover she could find .

Diya grew frustrated and not sure of what to do. She felt awkward in public , not quiet fitting in . Although Diya had missed human contact she found it overwhelming now that she could not just go home . Diya missed the Floras and her swing . She had found her way to the ocean , watching the sail ships coming in and out of the bay . The ocean made Diya feel at ease. She sat watching the waves roll over the top of the water , as if they were sweeping all her worries

away . For the first time in months Diya felt at
peace . She watched a ship come to dock , listening
to the men call orders back and forth . Then it
came to her . She would go out to sea ! Diya
frowned at the thought as she knew as a woman
she would not be allowed on the boat, unless they
didn't know she was a woman . Diya smiled in joy
at the idea . Standing up she made her way back to
town to find some proper man clothes .

Diya found some men's clothes off
of a clothes line in no time . She wrapped her hair
in a bandana and got dressed . Diya was excited ,
something she had not felt for a very long time .
She had gotten comfortable in her old life,
forgetting the feeling of surprise of the unknown .
Diya took a gulp of air as if it would give her
courage and headed back towards the ocean .

Bravely she walked up to the docks
and the ships attached to them . The sailors were
talking loudly between themselves , joking around ,
yelling insults back and forth at each other .

" Who goes there ? " yelled a man from atop one of the ships .

The crowd grew quiet and Diya realized that he was talking to her .

" Looking for work " replied Diya in the lowest voice she could muster , she stared at the dock in fear , waiting to be called out as a woman at any minute .

" Who ? " asked the man still yelling .

" Me ! " said Diya in her new low voice , louder this time .

The man started laughing .

" You are nothing but a bean pole and a boy from what I see " yelled the man .

The crowd of sailors gave a loud laugh at his response .

" I can work ! " said Diya stubbornly.

The man disappeared and then could be heard as he climbed down from the ship.

He was muttering away to himself .
Diya stood watching him and tried not to laugh . As
he got closer to her she saw that he was a beast of
a man . He towered over Diya , his arm as big as
Diya's waist . She gasped and then regained
herself .

" I need work " said Diya in her man
voice .

" They keep getting smaller ! What
are they feeding kids anymore ? " yelled the man to
the sailors as he look Diya up and down . The
sailors all started to laugh and agree with the man .

" Please sir " said Diya quietly.

" We do need someone to clean up
below don't we boys ? " said the man loudly .

The men nodded and gave a
chuckle .

" Get up on the ship . We own you
now boy " yelled the man in Diya's face .

Diya quickly ran over to the ship
and started climbing the ladder . She sighed in

relief and tried to hide her happiness.

The next couple months sucked . Diya was sick all of the time , she was put to work down below the deck . It was dark and smelled like urine . She had to clean , cook and kill rats . The ships captain deemed her to small of a man to be above deck to help . The men on board laughed and teased her for being so weak. Diya was stubborn and knew she would get her sea legs soon enough or at least she hoped . At night Diya would go up above to watch the moon . The swaying of the ship reminded her of her swing at home .

Diya learned and loved the ship life . She watched other sailors come and go but her captain stayed the same . Diya found ease in her new life . It was hard work but she was left to her own for the most part of it . Very few tried to talk to her . Diya was thankful as she thought her male voice was horrible so it was easier to just not talk .

At one of the ports she found a kitten

wandering on the shore line so out of place . Diya picked up the kitten and hid it in her shirt as she reboarded her ship . She named it Sandy since she had found him on the shores sand . By a fluke Sandy ended up growing up to be a big burly tomcat who loved hunting the rats on the ship. Diya spoiled her new friend and he spoiled her with his affection. He became apart of the ship and apart of Diya's heart .

The ship was called Ollera and was mainly used for transport . They spent months on end on the seas , sailing from one port to another . The captain was known as Redu, he was a fair man from what Diya seen . Redu had not spoken to Diya since the first day she had stepped on the ship . He would simply nod at Diya if they would make eye contact . She learned that the ship was known for being one of the fastest ships as well as one of the largest in the world . This made Diya proud to be apart of such a great ship . There were anywhere from 20 to 30 men on the boat at any given time . Some men would only make it one voyage before jumping off at the next port , some even kissing the ground swearing to the god's they would never set foot on a ship again . A lot of men never made it off the boat alive . Whether it was from sickness or injury , death seemed to be aboard as if it was a dear friend .

Diya watched in horror one day as a wave came out of no where and picked up 3 men off the deck as if they were matchsticks and carried them into the water to never be seen again . She learned to respect the water that surrounded them at all times . It was as if the sea was its own person with feelings who would get out of control. Like a angry toddler on some days and a sweet sweet lover on calm nights .

Fish was a main staple of food for the ship . Nets were set daily along their travels and would bring a variety of fish. Diya learned how to trade for other ingredients at any ports they stopped at . Once off the ship she was not afraid to ask locals how to properly make food or for any suggestions as to make her ship life easier . Diya learned a lot and applied her new skills to the ship. She constructed a small room with shelves to keep the food up from the floor and to keep dry. It also stopped other crew members from raiding the supplies in the middle of the night . She understood hunger but the food needed to last their voyages across the seas .

Diya loved the thrill of the sea . She welcomed the storms and the rocky waves . She witnessed dolphins as they swam beside the ship calling out as if they wanted her to join them . Whales that were beyond huge that swam with playful seals . The ocean had its own world with its own rules. Diya would always get excited seeing the seagulls after a long trip knowing that it meant that land was near by .

Very rarely on some nights the captain would sit and tell stories . These were Diya's favorite evenings of all . They would all sit while the captain would tower above them as he spun his tale . He would pace back and forth deep in thought as he gave his story life trough his booming voice . His voice was loud but soothing and before you knew it you were captivated . Some stories were happy or funny but mostly sad or gruesome in nature . Diya often wondered if he had a huge imagination or if he had indeed experienced each event personally .

One evening the captain started a story that Diya had never heard before . She sat down quickly to listen . Diya had already spent years on the boat and had thought she had already heard every tale to be told by the captain . Her faithful tomcat came right over and made himself at home on her lap purring loud as he made himself comfortable .

" Shhh sandy " Diya whispered into the cats ear .

Soon all the men sat and waited patiently for the captain to resume his tale .

" This is a true story passed onto me by my family and my family before " boomed the captain .

The night was calm and the stars were bright . Diya had no idea that this would now be her favorite story of all time as she leaned in to listen with cat in lap .

Chapter 10

" When the earth was young and barley any men walked the earth a race of people showed up from the heavens . They were said to have blue and green eyes , never seen before . " The captain paused and looked right at Diya before continuing .

" They were smart and educated people and said to have built a whole city in just one week . "

" That's not possible " said one of the men suddenly .

" But yet it was possible as they brought with them giants to be the builders " explained the captain with a sparkle in his eyes .

" Giants ?! " exclaimed the men almost in sync .

The captain smiled and nodded waiting for the men to settle back down . He continued on with his tale .

" They built a city in just one week . Grew gardens and made water come on demand . The land around them grew so many different plants and trees . They had many tools , some would even play music . These people from the heavens loved to laugh and dance . They would have many feasts and invite people from all around .They had special powers " The captain paused to take a swig of his wine knowing he had everyone's attention . Which he did .

Diya looked around at the men wide eyed waiting on his every word . She had to admit he was sounding pretty crazy but she to was curious as to where this was all going as she had never heard any mention of this race of people before .

" They had boxes they sat in and they would ..... " he paused again .

" The boxes would take them up in the air at their will . They could fly with the birds in the sky "

Some of the men broke out laughing.

" I lie not " Boomed the captain .

The men stopped laughing as they realized the captain was not joking but serious in his story .

" These people from the heavens brought animals we had never seen before . Some were part man and part horse . Some were furry little dogs that could also fly "

Diya froze . Furry little dogs that could fly ? Did he mean the Floras ? She held her breath in excitement .

" Decades went by and people from all around came and settled around the city . The people from the heavens spread out to all corners of the earth . Teaching everyone a new way of life . It was a grand time full of harmony for all . "

" Then one day the skies opened above and started raining , the ground below them grumbled and roared , smoke came out of cracks that had magically appeared in the ground overnight . The rain did not stop . The sun had went away and was replaced by only darkness . Then one night the earth grew angry and the water started to boil . The earth split open and water came from everywhere flooding out the city . Water covered almost every part of the earth . Many died and others ran to the tops of the tallest mountains and survived to share the story . The rain lasted for 92 days and then stopped . The city that had once been full and alive was now no where to be seen underneath a ocean of new water . The people from the heavens had almost but all disappeared . Some saying that they had went in their fancy boxes and flew back up to their heaven home . " The captain paused to take another long drink of his wine .

" This story has been told through my family for as long as my family has been alive . It has been told that some people from the heavens did not leave but stayed here on earth to help us . If you should happen to meet a person with the blue or green eyes then you know they are bloodlines of the people from the heavens " The captain again paused and looked at Diya as if to make a point .

The captain lit his pipe and took a long draw . The men started to get up and mutter in between themselves . Diya sat unmoving still with cat in lap , she looked up to the night sky in bewilderment . She had never heard of these people from the heavens . Diya had read many books throughout her long life , but not one mentioned this race of people . Were these her people she suddenly wondered . A star shot across the sky as if it was some magic answer to her hidden question .

" Boy " said the captain suddenly .

Diya jumped in surprise and dropped Sandy on the deck floor . He gave her a rude look as he slowly made his way across the ships deck carefully avoiding any puddles of water as his soft paws hit the floor .

" Yes captain ? " answered Diya quietly watching Sandy zig zag across the deck .

" You ever hear this tale before ? " asked the captain curiously .

" No captain " answered Diya thoughtfully .

" But your eyes " said the captain with a sense of urgency .

Diya quickly made eye contact with the captain and then shifted her gaze to the deck once again as if he would see all her truth if they held the gaze .

" Come closer " said the captain almost whispering .

Diya turned and started to walk away . She did not want to go closer to the captain .

" Boy !! " exclaimed the captain .

Diya stopped walking .

110

" Come here now ! " exclaimed the captain this time with a hint of anger in his voice .

Diya turned and cautiously walked over to where the captain was sitting . The night sky was starting to eagerly blow the water around them . She looked up and saw the clouds coming in from the east , dark and blocking out the moon light .

" Look at me " asked the captain .

Diya lifted her head slowly and made eye contact with the captain . He had huge dark brown eyes . Almost chestnut in color .

" Well call me a clam " exclaimed the captain suddenly and he broke out with laughter .

Diya was caught by surprise . What was he laughing about ?

" You're a girl ! " exclaimed the captain .

Diya's face instantly turned red .

" No ! " said Diya in her man voice .

" Oh yes you are " said the captain as he reached out to grab at her clothing . Diya stepped back .

" Oh you're a cheeky one , come here girl " said the captain as he reached out again to grab Diya's arm .

Diya took another step back .

" Where are you going ? " said the captain with a burst of laughter .

Diya looked around the boat in panic . The wind had picked up and was smashing water against the boat as if it was a child throwing a fit . As if on cue water started pouring from the dark night sky . The captain raised to his feet and slowly started walking towards Diya . With every step he took towards her she took a step back .

" To think all these lonely years and here I have a girl right here with me " said the captain . He stopped and looked up to the night sky.

" Thank you gods for this gift ! "

yelled the captain in joy to his invisible gods . The

sky lit up with a lighting bolt hitting the water as if

to answer his call . Diya screamed , surprised by

the random lighting strike .

" Come on girl ! Quit playing ! "
yelled the captain as he continued walking towards

Diya .

Diya realized she had no where else

to go , she was backed up against the bow of the

boat . Looking behind her she could only see the

darkness of the night , water splattered her face as

the wind blew . Another bolt of lighting hit the

water , this time closer to the boat . It lit up the

sky , Diya could see the determination on the

captains face as he moved closer and closer to her .

" Stay back " screamed Diya .

" Or what ? " screamed the captain .

Diya grabbed the edge of the boat

and swung herself up to stand on the wooden

railing . The captain stopped and then started

laughing again . The wind was blowing so hard now

that it picked up his hat and stole it away into the night . He didn't seem to notice as he laughed , his eyes more on the prize , a woman , his own .

" Come down from there girl , you are going to hurt yourself . I am not going to harm you " said the captain calmly and he extended his hand to Diya .

The storm gave a sigh and then seemed to exhale all its rage . Diya felt a surge of fear run through her body . Looking at the captain she could see him standing on the deck feet away from her , unbothered by the storm , hand out , waiting . A wave came out of nowhere and hit the boat hard , Diya screamed again and reached out to grab the captains hand . The wave picked her up and swept her out to sea , leaving the captain standing with eyes wide in amazement , hand still held out .

Chapter 11

Diya had lost count of how many days she had been in the sea . The last thing she remembered was reaching for the captains hand before she was taken by the wind and water . The wave had picked her up as if she was a piece of sand and carried her in to the oceans depths .

She awoke to floating in the water , looking around all she could see was the ocean . No life . No boat . Nothing but water . Diya had lost count of how many times she had taken on water and drowned . The most horrible way to die as far as she was concerned . It was slow and painful . What was more painful was waking back up , still floating in the water with no land in sight . Swimming seemed to be useless as it felt like she was going no where . Her clothes slowly started to fall apart , her skin becoming so wrinkled from the constant salt water . Diya's lips cracked and bled and her voice crackled whenever she tried to yell or even whisper . Death was her only consistent .

It was not always drowning . Sharks were everywhere and she was easy bait . She would welcome the sharks sometimes knowing that it would be a quick death with them tearing her apart . Diya would hope that she would awake on land or perhaps a boat . Sharks were not the only enemy in the huge ocean . Jellyfish would swim by the hundreds together and at times she would float into them causing her to be stung hundreds of times . Once a whale came up and swallowed her whole much to her surprise . Diya had always wanted to see a whale up close but this was over the top . The ocean was full of curious creatures all wanting to harm Diya in one way or another . She always awoke though , still floating , surrounded by water with no land in sight .

Diya called for the Flora's , she called for God . No one came to save her . It was just her and the sea . She prayed for death . She tried bargaining with God and then the Devil . But no one ever showed up . It did not take long for her to lose count of the days. Diya cried until she could cry no more finally understanding what hell actually felt like .

Days turned into nights and nights turned into weeks . Diya no longer had any clothes , seaweed covered her body now as she floated randomly . Her face swollen from no water and her lips blistered from the sun . At times she would welcome the death just to wake up feeling refreshed for a short time before the horror story she was living would restart .

Then one day she awoke , not in water but on a hard surface . She could hear a man yelling .

" IT'S A MERMAID !! "

117

Opening her eyes she could see a group of men standing over top of her staring wide eyed . Looking around she saw that she was in a huge fish net .

" IT IS ALIVE ! " screamed another man in horror .

Before Diya could look up at the man she felt a sharp pain across her head and everything went dark .

This time waking up was different . Diya could feel bedding underneath her and a blanket covering her . She gave a silent sigh and slowly opened her eyes . To her surprise she was in a room all tucked into a bed . Looking over herself she could see all the seaweed was gone and she was in a white cotton dress . Diya smiled and stretched out her limbs .

" Hello " said a female voice from the corner of the room .

Diya jumped in surprise and then saw where the voice had come from .

There sitting in the corner of the room was a lady on a chair . She looked to be in her thirties , dressed very well with a smile on her face . Diya rubbed her eyes in disbelief and watched the lady get up and walk across the room towards her .

" My name is Ruth and you are on the ship Christoff my darling " said Ruth as she stopped in front of Diya and bent over to run her hand through Diya's hair .

Diya remained unmoving watching Ruth in surprise .

" You must be in shock . The men thought they had found themselves a mermaid " said Ruth laughing .

" A mermaid ! Oh what imagination those young fools have . I don't know how you survived the hit to your head " said Ruth as she continued to run her hand through Diya's hair .

" Not a mark on you ! Arthor hit you pretty hard with the shovel . You scared him I must say ! But he must hit like a girl because I can not find any mark on your pretty head " explained Ruth as pulled her hand away from Diya's head .

Ruth suddenly grabbed Diya's hands and knelt beside the bed .

" Lets pray . It is a miracle that you are alive . Lord thank you for this life . Blessed you are to have such miracles happen . Amen " whispered Ruth into their clasped hands . She jumped back up and let go of Diya's hands .

Diya stared wide eyed at Ruth . She was unable to think of anything to say . She had never met anyone like this Ruth before . Usually the ladies she had met had very little to say and if they did it was not very much . But Ruth flowed both with speech and held herself as if she had rights like a man . She reminded Diya of herself before her first death . Full of life and opinions .

" Do you even speak ? I wonder where you came from and those marks all over your body " said Ruth as she paused to run her hand down Diya's arm . Diya pulled back her arm in surprise , she had not had anyone touch her for hundreds of years .

"I did not mean to scare you " said Ruth softly looking into Diya's eyes .

Diya felt a tear run down her cheek . She had not felt such warmth from another human for so long .

"Oh darling " said Ruth as she wiped away the tear .

"You are safe now ! " exclaimed Ruth with a huge smile .

Diya smiled back , still not sure of what to say in response .

The door to the cabin gave a loud knock . Ruth walked over and opened the door slowly .

"Yes ? " said Ruth .

"Well ? " asked a voice on the other side of the door . Diya could tell it was a man .

"Well what ? " asked Ruth .

" Is she ? " the man whispered as he tried to peek his head into the room . Ruth pushed him out before he could lay eyes on Diya . She rolled her eyes before answering the man .

" Good god are you a dummy ? " said Ruth .

" They still think you are a mermaid ! Silly silly men " whispered Ruth to Diya as she shut the door firmly . She walked back over to Diya and sat down on the edge of the bed . Ruth stared at Diya for a minute before continuing on with her one sided conversation .

" I wonder where you have come from my lovely . You look like you are ... lets say in your twenties . I can tell you were taking care of . Do you even speak ? I have to assume you are a slave , you must be with all those marks on your body . My poor poor girl . " said Ruth as she looked at Diya with big wide eyes . Diya thought for a minute she might even start crying .

" Well today your life changes !! "

Exclaimed Ruth as she suddenly jumped up from the bed and swirled around the room as if she could hear music playing somewhere in the distance .

" I am Ruth Digeo , my husband is the famous Direk Digeo . We are some of the richest people in the world my darling . I am not bragging just telling you facts . To be honest I don't even know if you can understand me , but we will work on that . " said Ruth as she stopped just as suddenly as she had started and bent over to look Diya in her eyes . Ruth's eyes sparkled with Joy .

" You are on our ship , so lucky the men found you really . So many ships out there full of scandalous criminals who would have ... " said Ruth who seemed to get lost in thought .

Diya watched Ruth . She was a pretty woman who seemed to be so full of life . Her features were soft and she could tell that Ruth had probably never worked a day in her life . She filled the room with her personality . Diya liked her .

" So you will be my hand maid "
said Ruth with a big smile .

Diya frowned at the word maid .

" Oh you don't like that word ?
Hand maid ? " said Ruth carefully watching Diya
for a reaction .

" That's fine . You will be my
person . Do you like that better ? I have no friends
where we are going . I will know no one ! You will
help me with whatever I need help with , be by
myside at all times . I am not a savage I can assure
you ! I will pay you and teach you how to read ,
write , be a proper lady " said Ruth with
excitement . She started nodding her head and
then reached out to gently move Diya's head to nod
in agreement . Diya gave a unexpected giggle at
Ruth's random behaviour .

" Oh good ! You agree " exclaimed
Ruth in glee as she walked across the room to the
door and opened it .

" I feel better now that we have had

this talk . You better rest some more , we have another couple days until we reach ... oh wait I did not even tell you where we are going ? " said Ruth as she looked thoughtful once again and laughed to herself .

" We are going to Venice darling ! " said Ruth as she left the room shutting the door behind her . The room seemed painfully silent with her departure .

Chapter 12

The next couple days went by fast .
Diya was soon well rested and fed . Ruth grew on
her more and more as each day passed . Diya
decided it was best if perhaps she did not talk for
awhile . Ruth had no problem with doing all the
talking it seemed . Diya loved Ruth's constant
chitter chatter . Plus she did not want to try and
explain herself to Ruth . The story of being a slave
seemed much more believable then the truth . Ruth
was very kind and Diya felt as if she could trust
her . Soon she was following Ruth around the boat
eagerly listening to her every word . Diya was
excited to be seeing Venice . She had heard from
all around the country about the magical city built
on the water .

" You are doing so well " said Ruth
as she sat down at the table in the makeshift
kitchen on the ship . Diya sat down as well and
nodded at Ruth with a smile .

" I just know that you can
understand me ! " said Ruth as she winked at
Diya . Her husband Direk walked in and sat down
giving Ruth a warm smile . He looked over at Diya
briefly and then turned his attention to his wife .

" How is your mermaid doing ? "
asked Direk with a chuckle .

" You're a funny man my husband !
She is no mermaid ! She is a girl , whole with no
tail I can promise you " replied Ruth smiling .

" Something smells fishy here " said
Direk still chuckling at his own humour .

" That would be you ! " said Ruth
laughing as she gently poked her husband in his
side with her finger . He grabbed her finger and
swiftly brought it up to his lips and kissed it
tenderly . Ruth blushed instantly . Diya could

127

see the love between these two and instantly adored both of them . She had learned that Direk was a antique dealer for the church . The church would pay him to collect all artifacts that could be found . This made Diya very happy as she was excited to get back into a church . It had been way to long . The Digeo's were good people and Ruth had been right , Diya was very lucky indeed to have been found by them . The right place at the right time with the right people . Maybe god had a purpose for her after all .

Within days the buildings on the water showed up . It was early one morning . Diya was up on deck watching the water as the sun rose . The water was engulfed in fog and the sun was trying to break through its thick dense air . Then she saw the first . It was grand as it peeked through the fog at Diya . She gasped at the size of the building , as they got closer she could see it was a huge castle sitting on the water . Then another showed up and another . Each one more amazing then the last . Each adorned with statues , glassware and fancy patterns . Diya sat wide eyed as the ship silently floated by each one . A horn went off in the distance and the men quickly worked to drop the anchor .

" Ready ? " whispered Ruth .

Diya jumped in surprise . She had not heard Ruth approach her . She quickly stood up and nodded yes . Diya followed Ruth as she climbed down the side of the ship into a small thin boat . A man silently stood on the one end with a huge paddle . Ruth patted the seat next to her and as soon as they sat down the man started paddling them away in the thick fog . Within minutes they were at a dock and onto a cobblestone walk way .

" Follow close , there are many bridges and alleys here , with this fog it can be easy to get lost here " said Ruth as she started walking . Diya followed closely as they made their way along the walk way . The air was thick of the grey fog . Looking up she could see the shadows of giant buildings pop in and out of sight . Almost as they were shadows playing in the morning sun . They rounded a corner and before them was a huge courtyard surrounded by these ghostly buildings . Diya's eyes grew wide and she stopped walking to absorb all the beauty around her .

" Eyes down and hurry up " whispered Ruth suddenly seeming to appear out of nowhere . Diya nodded and followed Ruth . She came to a door that looked like a giant would fit through and knocked softly . The door opened immediately and they were beckoned to come in . As soon as they enter Diya realized they were in a church . She had never seen a church like this before . Gold was everywhere , gold paintings , gold railings and if it was not gold it was the color of gold . It took a minute for her eyes to adjust to the brightness of what seemed like a cavern of god . Ruth grabbed her elbow and gently steered Diya into a side room .

" I will be back . Just stay here "

whispered Ruth as she quickly turned around and left . Diya watched Ruth leave and wished she could continue by her side to explore all the treasures beyond the small room she was in . Looking around she realized that this must be a servant waiting area as it was full of young girls and boys waiting patiently . Diya found a seat in the corner and sat down .

" Are you the mermaid girl ? " whispered a young girl from beside her . She had golden blonde hair that almost seemed to glow and a sparkle in her eyes that Diya had not seen for a long time .

" Yes " whispered Diya back leaning over . The girls eyes widened and she turned to the girl on her other side and said a loud told you so . The girl rolled her eyes and looked away . Seeming proud she turned back and looked Diya up and down .

" You seem pretty old for a mermaid " whispered the blonde hair girl .

" Old ? I am barely 22 " whispered Diya trying not to laugh out loud .

" That is pretty old . Where is your tail ? " said the girl looking at Diya's feet sadly .

" I only have a tail when I am in the sea " replied Diya smartly .

" I thought you couldn't talk ? " asked the girl looking closer at Diya .

" Only special people can hear me " answered Diya back smiling .

The girls eyes widened and started to sparkle again .

" My name is Paige " said the girl suddenly sticking out her hand for Diya to shake . Diya took her little hand and they did a little hand shake .

" My name is Diya " said Diya .

" Diya . What a pretty name " said Paige softly .

The door opened and Ruth peeked her head in . She beckoned to Diya to follow .

Diya got up and waved goodbye to her new friend Paige .

" I really have to give you a name , I can not just keep calling you like some sort of animal " said Ruth as they left the church . Diya tried not to laugh as Ruth kept muttering to herself as they walked along the boardwalk . Diya was not sure why she continued her silence with Ruth but felt in her gut it was the best thing to do .

They spent a week there and then it was off to the New World . It would be 7 months before Diya would see her new friend and be able to converse . This pattern went on for years that turned into decades . Diya learned that her ship was one that transported for the church . Mostly gold and precious metals . The ship was one of the fastest on the seas . Ruth and her husband were well known and trusted in all church circles . Diya felt completely at home in her new surroundings .

Paige would always be at the dock awaiting Diya's return . She would run up and grab

Diya and hug her tight . She was there every time without fail . As the years went by Diya watched Paige turn into a young lady , get married and have her own babies . Paige never questioned why Diya never aged she would only fill Diya in on what she had missed while she was gone . Life was as perfect as Diya could ask for .

Then one day Ruth passed on . Diya had spent over 50 years by her side , she was not surprised as she realized that Ruth had grown quite old . What did surprise Diya was the auction and how she was a part of it .

Chapter 13

Ruth and her husband never had any children . When Ruth died the church took all their belongings and put it up for auction , including Diya , as she was property of Ruth therefore now property of the church . Church officials came and collected Diya that very same day to be held at the church until said auction . Diya sat quietly in the same room she had met Paige so many years before . Looking around she realized the room was like her , never changing even though time marched on . She wondered if she should start planning her escape soon as she did not want to be owned by anyone else in her lifetime . The door to the room slowly opened and a older gentleman slowly walked in shutting the door quietly . He shuffled over to Diya and sat down beside her .

" So you're a mermaid ? " asked the old man as he adjusted his long robe to sit straight . Diya had not been asked that for a long time and was taken by surprise not sure if she should answer .

" I was a young boy when you first appeared here , I know you can talk " said the old man . Diya looked around the room in a panic . She was not sure where he was going with this knowing the church did not approve of what they considered a abomination .

" All in due time my dear " said the old man almost in a whisper .

" I am in charge of the library here " said the old man . Diya looked up at him and then looked back down at the ground .

" Well that got a response . I am going to put in a bid to keep you here , to help with the library . Would you like that ? " asked the old man smiling now that he knew he had Diya's attention . Diya nodded yes .

" See you soon " said the old man getting up from the chair . He left the room at the same slow pace without a goodbye or even looking back . As the door shut Diya let out a breath of air .

Several hours had past and Diya was just about to fall asleep in the chair when the door opened once again . This time it was a young man looking impatient .

" Come with me " he said abruptly .

Diya stood up and walked over . He simply turned and started to walk away . He walked at a fast pace and started weaving his way through the large church . Through one chapel down a staircase to come out another door through another court yard . Diya had not realized exactly how large the church and all its chapels were . After more then twenty minutes they turned a corner and were in heaven .

Diya stopped in shock and felt amazement looking at the room . It was taller then the trees with shelves all the way to a glass ceiling full of books . Fancy ladders ran along the shelving on rollers . To Diya this was heaven . She could not count how many books were in the room . She smiled at her luck . This was exactly were she wanted to be .

" Never seen a library before ? " asked the young man sarcastically .

Diya looked at him and frowned . He was kind of a jerk she thought to herself as she looked back up to the glass ceiling .

" Daniel ! You have found her . Thank you " said the old man walking over to them .

" Of course priest " replied Daniel as he kneeled .

" I can see that you like the library " said the old man to Diya .

Diya again nodded in response .

" Let me introduce myself properly .
I am priest Hathor . I was appointed a very long
time ago to be master of the library for the church .
What is your name ? " asked Hathor very politely .

" Diya " said Diya suddenly . She
felt like she could trust Hathor even if she had just
met him hours before .

" The light , very good " said Hathor
quickly as he smiled even bigger .

" Sir ? " asked Daniel .

" Yes ? " said Hathor breaking his
gaze from Diya to look at Daniel .

" Why is she here ? I am not trying
to be rude or disrespectful . I am just curious as to
why you would have me bring someone like her
down here to such a precious place ? " asked
Daniel .

" Someone like her ? " asked Hathor
losing the smile off of his face .

" I did not mean it like that sir "
said Daniel blushing .

" She belongs to the church Daniel .
This is her home now . You should feel lucky to
have her here with us , I am sure she will be of
great help . Now show her to her room and you are
done for the day . " said Hathor firmly .

" Yes sir " said Daniel .

" Diya . We will see you in the
morning " said Hathor the smile once again
returning to his face .

Daniel started out of the room and
Diya quickly followed . It was only a couple of turns
and down a hallway before they were in front of a
row of doors .

" The third door is your room " said
Daniel almost sounding mad .

" Did I do something wrong ? "
asked Diya suddenly .

Daniel shot her a look before
answering as if he was choosing his words
carefully .

" I am here to take over the library

when Hathor passes it on . You are just here to help . Don't forget your place " answered Daniel as he opened the first door and disappeared into the room .

Diya loved her new life . She would work dawn till dusk everyday in the library . She was allowed to take books to her room every night as long as they were back in the morning . Hathor was in joy when she asked to borrow the books almost jumping in excitement at the very fact she could read . Diya lived and breathed the library . When she was not in the library she was also allowed to visit one of the chapels to pray . It was a great honor she knew and she took advantage of it every moment that she could .

Diya would see Paige and her family every month . It saddened her to watch Paige grow old , her children now having their own babies . Paige's family always welcomed Diya with wide arms and happiness , often referring to her as the mermaid , never questioning . Diya had never felt apart of a family until Paige and loved her dearly for sharing hers with no judgement . It was a warm fall day when Paige passed on . The funeral was full of her children and grandchildren , Diya right by their side . She cried that day for the loss of her friend . Someone who had never had any judgement or fear towards her , nothing but unconditional love . After a hundred lifetimes Diya also knew how rare people like Paige were . As the funeral ended Diya noticed Daniel standing back off in the corner . He had also grown since she had first met him , but still had the same scowl on his face that she remembered from the first day .

" Diya " said Daniel as they made eye contact and he motioned her over to him . Diya made her way through the crowd of people stopping in front of Daniel .

" Why do you never age ? " whispered Daniel looking Diya up and down .

" Excuse me ? " said Diya surprised .

" Why do you never seem to age ? "
asked Daniel .

" I don't know ? " answered Diya
defensively .

" There is something off about you
Diya . I have known it from day one . Something
evil . " said Daniel as he walked away . Diya stood
there speechless unsure of how to respond to his
statement .

Diya spent even more time in the
chapel praying to God . She did not feel evil but still
wondered why God allowed to her to continue
living . At first she thought it was a punishment
and now she wondered if she indeed had some
greater purpose . Why would God keep bringing
her back to his home if she was evil , this made no
sense to her . She had almost read every book in
the library but had not read anything about anyone
like her . One night she was awoken very late ,
Hathor was not doing well . Diya figured he must
be close to a hundred in age by now . She made her

way to his room . He was surrounded by priests
chanting prayers while candles lit up the room .

" Leave " said Hathor to the priests .
They nodded and left the room leaving Diya
standing there looking at Hathor wide eyed .

" Come closer Diya " said Hathor
softly . Diya grabbed a chair and sat down next to
Hathor as he lay on his bed . She grabbed his
hand and squeezed it tightly .

" I am going to pass soon Diya "
whispered Hathor . Diya could hear him gasp for
air as he spoke . She tried to hide back her tears of
sadness . It felt like they had just met and here
she was saying goodbye much to soon .

" I want you to take over the library
Diya " said Hathor in a strong voice .

" But what about Daniel ? " asked
Diya surprised .

" He has no love for the books . Not
like you my star child " answered Hathor weakly
as he smiled at Diya .

" I have left all the proper

paperwork . The church has approved you Diya "

said Hathor gasping again for air .

" Thank you so much Hathor . I do

love the books . I will take very good care of the

library " whispered Diya . She was amazed . She

had never even considered running the library .

Hathor gasped one last time and then the room

went silent . Diya sat silently with tears running

down her face . Another great soul gone . She heard

someone come in the room and turned to find

Daniel standing there with arms wide open . Diya

stood up and hugged Daniel tightly , he hugged her

back .

" He has passed " whispered Diya

into Daniels ear as he held her .

" I know I heard everything " he

whispered into Diya's ear .

" He was a great man " whispered

Diya as tears still ran down her face and now onto

Daniels shoulder .

" Yes he was " whispered Daniel and he stepped back to look Diya in her eyes .

Diya looked up at Daniel and saw a tear running down his face . She reached up and wiped it away with her hand . Then she felt a shearing pain in her side . Looking down she could see Daniel stabbing her with a knife . Blood was everywhere . Diya grabbed her side and tried to stop Daniel .

" Why ? " whimpered Diya as blood poured out of her onto the floor . She fell to her knees .

" It is my library not yours Diya . I told you that years ago . But you did not listen . You followed Hathor around like a lost dog . Did you think the you would run the library ? " said Daniel as he stood above her with so much anger .

Diya passed out on the floor . Daniel picked her up and threw her out the window claiming she had jumped out when Hathor had died .

Chapter 14

Diya awoke two days later and found herself in a heap of discarded bodies in a field . The smell made her start dry heaving as she moved rotten body parts off of her to find her way out of the carnage . Once free , Diya let out a scream full of anger and sadness . She knew what she had to do , move on as always . Part of her wanted to go back and confront Daniel but she knew it would cause more trouble then anything . Diya hated moving on as she for the first time in a thousand years she had truly felt like she had a home . She knew Daniel had in some twisted way done her a favor . The years would pass by and if not Daniel it would have been some other faithful servant or priest that would have noticed Diya who never aged . Looking up to the sky Diya said a prayer asking god which way to go . A black raven appeared suddenly above her head , cooing a soft song . Diya cooed back and smiled . She watched the bird fly off , knowing which way she should go .

Diya made her way across Europe , slowly but surely as the years passed by . She was always able to find work and if she could choose it would be in a library . Her love for books never stopped . Diya knew every novel ever written and was excited when she found new literature to read . The words star child were stuck in her head . Hathor had called her this before he passed . Was he trying to tell her something she did not know ? It was another 300 years before she heard the name again .

Diya had found a settlement deep in the country side . As she traveled she avoided the bigger towns and groups of people . War seemed to be breaking out everywhere around her . The world was at a breaking point . She still prayed everyday for god to show her what her purpose was or to just let her die . At this point she would take either with welcoming arms .

" Girl are you lost ? " asked a man suddenly . Diya looked up and caught her breath . Standing before her was the most handsome man she had ever laid eyes on . He towered over Diya with the softest green eyes staring warmly down at her . Diya felt flustered and unable to speak at first . He waited patiently for her answer .

" Girl ? " he asked again this time with some concern .

" Yes ? " answered Diya finally .

" You are lost ? " asked the man .

" No " answered Diya quickly .

The man started to laugh .

" So your not lost ? " asked the man with a smile .

" I am looking for work " answered Diya quietly .

" Are you now ? " said the man .

149

Diya was not sure if he was being sarcastic or genuine .

" The third house on the right , May is always looking for help . " said the man as he pointed towards the house .

" Thank you " said Diya .

The man gave a bow and walked away leaving Diya standing there watching him with amazement . She had never felt this way around another person at all , it was as if he had awoken something that had been dead all these years . He was right . May was a older woman who did need help . She was a baker and supplied the area with baked goods . May was overjoyed when Diya asked for work as she had been alone for years with no help . Diya instantly like May , she was a simple lady and Diya appreciated it . May gave Diya her own room , fed her and even gave her a percentage of sales . It was one of Diya's favorite memories over her long life . She learned how to bake with May . Rising every morning at the crack of dawn and working until it was to

dark to see . It was keeping the fire going ,

collecting grains from the fields , trading with other

people for missing ingredients . Diya respected May

for how hard of a worker she was , she had never

realized until now how much work went into just

one loaf of bread . May was quiet with a quick

sense of humour . Diya instantly felt welcomed ,

not only by May but the community that

surrounded them .

Diya also learned that the man she

had first seen was named Darius . He lived on the

edge of town and was barely seen by anyone . He

preferred solitude . He had remained single for as

long as anyone had ever known . She had almost

forgotten about him with her new busy life . Then

one day she awoke to a single red rose left at the

doorstep . She cautiously bent over and picked up

the rose and opened the card addressed to her . It

had a heart drawn on the inside signed by Darius .

Looking around he was no where to be found .

Everyday for months , rain or sun , a single red rose would be on the doorstep for Diya . She found it curious that she had not seen him since the first meeting and did not know if she should seek him out or just wait for him to appear . For the first time in her life she was genuinely intrigued by a man . A year to the day, she awoke one morning and excitedly went to the doorstep to collect her rose . She opened the door to find Darius standing there , smile on his face with rose in hand . They stood there for a minute just smiling at each other and then he put his hand out for her . Diya grabbed it eagerly and followed Darius down the road .

From that day forward Diya spent every free moment with Darius . They consumed each other with every minute . Never in her life did she think this kind of love existed . Diya had read stories but nothing compared to the feelings she had when Darius came into view . They would talk into the early morning hours . Never a awkward moment between them , almost completing each

others sentences . He was very knowledgeable ,

having read as many books as Diya . His parents

had died young and left him with a huge house

and more money then he knew what to do with . He

had stayed single for so long as he found no grace

or conversation with the ladies in the area . He was

also shy at moments which sent Diya over the edge

of how much she could love someone . Twenty

years went by without notice . May died one early

morning . She was well in her sixties and had lived

well past her time . Diya dug a hole , buried her

and said a prayer for May knowing she was in a

much better place now .

She moved in with Darius and

they were happier then any happiness she had

ever know . Diya loved Darius's family home . It

was almost the size of a castle with 10 rooms

including a full library , balcony and ballroom . Of

course the library was Diya's favorite place of all .

She was surprised that they had a library , she was

even more surprised at what types of books filled
it . Hundreds of books on the sky and stars .
Hundreds more on the dark arts and occult .
Almost every book in the library was new to Diya
and there were well over a thousand books in the
collection . Diya felt like a kid in a candy store and
would smile every time she had a chance to go and
read . The library was in the shape of a octogen
with walls that were covered with books . The
ceiling was a huge skylight with plants hanging
down randomly . It became Diya's home quickly .

They never left the house . There
was no need to as Darius was also a skilled
hunter . The two made a unbeatable pair in the
forest . Diya would set traps and Darius would
hunt for Boar . They had a nice garden and Diya
baked anything that they needed . The days
blended into each other with ease . Darius had
woken up one morning and dropped to one knee
proudly holding a gold ring for Diya . No words
were said as he slipped the ring onto her finger and

they sealed the bond with a kiss . From that day forward Diya held her head a little higher as she was someone's wife now . Something she thought would never happen . She felt so complete .

Another 20 years slipped by . You could see the lines and wrinkles around Darius's face . Diya thought he was just as handsome as the day they had met . One evening he sat down beside her and gently played with her hair . She smiled and loved his attention .

" Darling ? " asked Darius breaking the silence of the room .

" Yes? " replied Diya softly .

" Why do you never age ? " asked Darius .

Chapter 15

Diya froze for a minute in a panic .
Darius was over 60 years of age and here she was
still looking the exact same as the day they had
met . Darius had teased her before about her
looking so young as he aged and Diya would tease
him back telling him that he clearly needed
glasses .

" Are you a star child ? " asked
Darius .

" I don't know ! " exclaimed Diya in
a harsh whisper . She looked away unsure of what
to do . Diya had never told a soul about her truth ,
she had always just ran .

" Have you made it to the top of that
book case ? " asked Darius as he pointed to a tall

bookcase standing by itself in the corner .

" No . Why ? " asked Diya looking
over at the bookcase .

" How old are you ? " asked Darius .

" I have lost count , over a thousand
years I know as much " whispered Diya . Darius's
eyes widened and he gave a laugh .

" Wow ! I was not expecting that "
said Darius .

Darius explained to Diya that he
knew she was different from the moment they had
met . He claimed the markings all over body gave it
away . Diya pulled away and he smiled reassuring
her that he loved her no matter pulling her closer .
Darius kissed her neck softly and worked his way
to her lips . Even at his age his arms were strong
and held her tight . Diya would always melt in his
arms . Darius was the only lover Diya had ever
known . He was gentle but rough at the same time .
He would not only ravage her body at times but
her mind as well .

That night he kissed every inch of her body and took her to places unknown in her mind . When they had finished they lay in a heap on the library tile staring at the night sky up above .

" What is a star child ? " whispered Diya into the night .

" A child born from the stars " whispered back Darius .

Diya turned to look at Darius . His handsome face etched out by the moonlight . He looked so peaceful , he turned to look at Diya .

" Have you died before ? " asked Darius suddenly serious .

" Yes . To many times " answered Diya thoughtfully .

" You are always reborn , the same as before ? " asked Darius still with a serious tome .

" Yes . Except for these markings . They are there when I awake " answered Diya as she looked down at her arm full of swirling black marks .

" You are chosen " said Darius .

" What ? " said Diya confused .

" To do gods work . You have been chosen ." said Darius .

" To do what ? I don't understand . This feels more like a curse . " said Diya sadly .

" To live a thousand lives ? You are so blessed ! " exclaimed Darius .

" It is a lonely existence " said Diya .

" Do you believe in god ? " asked Darius .

" You know I do " answered Diya .

" Then you know he has a plan for you " said Darius .

" To live forever ? Travel the lands with no friends or family ? I don't understand what he wants from me " said Diya sounding defeated .

" You will know when it happens " said Darius as he bent over and kissed Diya .

" How do you know so much ? "
asked Diya now curious .

" That bookshelf , the leather bond
book on the top is all about star children . A fable it
is said . I read it many times as a child and dreamt
of meeting one . You are exactly as the book
described " explained Darius smiling at Diya .

" Interesting " said Diya looking
back at the bookshelf .

" Now tell me darling " said Darius
serious again .

" Tell you what ? " answered Diya .

" What's the weirdest way you have
died ? " asked Darius trying not to laugh .

" You are a odd odd man ! " replied
Diya laughing .

They spent the night talking . Diya
explained the hundreds of ways she had died as
Darius listened . It felt good to actually tell her
truth . She felt safe and trusted Darius . They
laughed for most of the night and then held each

other tight as the morning sun peeked into the library . Diya slept so peacefully that night and dreamt of her long lost friends . It was as if she could know forgive all the wrongs done against her . Letting it all go with every word to Darius .

The leather bond book was a giant book . It was as Darius had said . It had no name , no date or any indication of who had written it . Diya turned each page slowly and carefully as the book was old . The pages were yellow and tattered at the edges . It was more like a guide book then anything . What was more interesting was the fact it said star children , indicating that there were more like her . Diya had never considered the fact that she was not alone . The book even explained how to win over a star child , a single red rose at their doorstep for a year . She chuckled as it had indeed worked . Her furry flying friends were even mentioned saying they were protectors of star children . Diya paused as she had not thought about them for a long time , a piece of such a

long life . Diya read the book over and over ,
looking for any other clues . She felt better
knowing that she did have a purpose and it was
gods work , now just to figure out what , when and
where ? Faith . That's what Darius told her . To
have faith . He made it sound so simple .

It was a short ten years before
Darius died . It was unexpected but not a surprise
to Diya . He was just over 70 and had been not
doing well for the previous year . He had been
coughing up blood . She cried , she could not stop
crying . The grief that came with Darius passing
was nothing Diya had ever felt before . She knew
this day had been coming but she did not know the
amount of pain it would cause . Darius had also
known this day would come . He had left the house
and all belongings to Diya in his will . Darius had
no other family to speak of and Diya was proud to
have some where to call home . She buried Darius
in the front yard underneath his favorite tree . Diya
handmade a cross marker for Darius .

It was months before Diya was able to make it through a day without shedding a tear . She wandered through the house replaying memories with Darius losing herself in thought . Years again slipped by without notice as Diya became a ghost in her own house . She knew she had a purpose but felt so empty now without Darius . Diya had thought she knew about loneliness but was proved wrong . Life without Darius was truly lonely . She hated every moment .

Then one night she heard a knock at the front door . At first she thought she had imagined the noise , but then again , this time louder , knocking . She scrambled to her feet and ran to the door . Looking out the peek hole she could see no one . Puzzled she opened the door slowly and walked out to the front porch . It was a calm quiet night with a full moon lighting up the yard . The cross on Darius's grave seemed to glow . Seeing nothing Diya turned to walk back into the house when she heard a whistle clear in the night .

Diya froze . She knew that whistle .
Turning back around she gasped in surprise .
There were her furry friends , what the captain had
called Floras . Hundreds hovering in the sky . It
had been hundreds of years since she had seen
them . Diya had forgotten how absolutely beautiful
they were . She gave a quick whistle and they
assembled in formation . Diya jumped with joy .
They remembered her !

" Diya " said a familiar voice .

It was her original Flora friend .
Diya beamed with joy .

" You . Go . Now " said the Flora .

Chapter 16

Diya did as told and packed up her belongings . She sealed up the house as best as she could , not knowing when she would be back . Before leaving Diya sat down at Darius's grave .

" I love you , now and forever " whispered Diya as she patted his grave .

She heard the whistle in the distance and knew it was time to go . She had spent the night up with her friends . Watching them play and fly , talking as much as they could with her . She was not sure why they had been gone for so long and when she asked them they would simply change the subject . They were insistent that it was time for her to go , which made Diya believe it was her time to do whatever work

God had planned for her .

Diya spent days traveling across the country side with the Flora's company . She ended up in a small village that had a orphanage . Diya was over joyed . This must be the place she was meant to do gods work . She walked right up to the front door and knocked loudly . A small frail nun answered after a couple minutes and let Diya right in . The orphanage was indeed looking for help . The nun offered her a room and advised someone would be by in the morning to start her training . Within minutes there was a knock at the door , Diya answered it to find a young girl with a plate of food for her . She thanked the girl taking the plate eagerly as she was hungry . Diya sat down on the bed and started eating feeling very pleased with herself , and then she started choking on a piece of chicken , and died .

This carried on for decades . Diya would find some work that could or would help god and she would die within days . She was starting to feel cursed . She got a job at a small church and was crushed by a piano the next day . Diya would pick herself up and walk to the next town to try again . She got a job helping the sick in a hospital and got food poisoning and you guessed it , died within the week . It became a horrible cycle but Diya was stubborn and knew her purpose would eventually appear . It was as if god was pushing her away from all of Europe . War seemed to be around her even more then ever . Diya had no interest in any of it . Last she had heard it was around the 1600's . Time meant nothing to Diya anymore , she lived in her own world . The Flora's would come anytime Diya would call and that comforted her . They would bring her presents at times , gold and coins she could use to live . The Flora's would encourage her to keep on moving as if they knew her final destination . Diya appreciated the company as she missed Darius so much . Her heart was empty without his presence in her life . She could hear him in her head at times and at times memories of him ran down her face . He was her once in a lifetime love , her soulmate . Diya hoped that one day she would make god so happy he would let her die so she could be reunited with her love .

But instead here she was , making her way across Europe once again , being reborn again every week . It was starting to surprise Diya at how many ways a person could die . She had purposely killed herself in the beginning but had not done it on purpose for over a thousand years . She had to admit she was getting a little jumpy not really knowing what to expect every week .

Diya was on her way to Rome . She had heard the city had grown so much since she had last seen it . It felt like the right way to go so she followed her gut instinct . Finding a small stream on the way she stopped for a break . Diya whistled for the Flora's and waited patiently , but not a one appeared . Puzzled Diya whistled again , this time louder . A man stepped out from behind a bush suddenly and stared at Diya . At first Diya smiled and nodded at the man and then she realized something was wrong . He walked right over to her and punched her in the face .

Everything went dark .

Diya awoke to water spraying in her face . She gulped for air and tried to move but was pinned in a cage with a bunch of women . It was dark and water kept splashing her , she started shivering and could hear waves . She passed out . Diya was not sure of how long she was unconscious . When she awoke the next time the sun was blaring her in the face . It took a moment for her eyes to adjust . The lady next to her was sobbing . Looking around she saw that she was in a metal cage with other women on the deck of a ship . They were not the only ones . There were cages all around full of people . Some men , women and even children .

" What is this ? " asked Diya to the woman next to her . She did not even acknowledge

Diya and continued to sob .

" Hey ! " said Diya a little louder to the lady .

" Be quiet ! Your going to get us in trouble ! " said a lady across from Diya sternly .

" What is this ? " whispered Diya to the lady . The lady looked around before answering .

" Slave ship ! " whispered the lady back as if Diya was stupid .

Diya sat back in shock . She had heard of people being kidnapped and being sold as slaves but she never thought it was real .

" Where are we going ? " whispered Diya to the lady . The lady ignored her not making eye contact .

" Where are we GOING ? " said Diya louder this time . The lady looked at her with panic in her eyes .

" New World " she whispered scowling but Diya could see the fear in her eyes .

The cage rattled as it was hit with a piece of metal . Diya screamed in shock .

" NO TALKING " yelled a big burly man as he walked by .

The lady scowled at Diya .

The next year was one of the worst years of Diya's life . The men that had kidnapped them were truly savage .

Diya and her mates were never let out of the cage . They were given bare minimum to survive . Once a day a man would walk by and throw dry hard biscuits into each cage , another man would follow and pour water . Diya would cup her hands to catch as much as she could to eagerly drink it down . Each cage held 10 people , body to body with no room to move . It was a struggle . If you had to go to the bathroom , you went where you sat . There was no wiggle room to speak of . Within the first week the smell of urine was so strong across the deck . Diya welcomed the storms to clean off all the filth from her .

Every week that passed the nightmare continued and at times grew worse . Even though Diya welcomed the storms she also had learned to fear them . The cages were held on the deck with metal hooks , they were locked with big locks that needed a key . The previous week Diya had watched in horror as a storm picked up one of the cages and took it to sea . She cried for the people locked inside knowing they would quickly drown and sink to the bottom ocean floor never to be seen again . Diya did not fear death or the ocean , she feared being locked in a cage at the bottom of the sea for eternity . To be reborn to drown to be reborn again , it was a loop she never wanted to experience .

One by one people slowly died around her . That was the only time the cages were open , to discard of the bodies . The men running the boat would discard the bodies overboard , sometimes angry , complaining that these slaves were weak . If someone died they would leave them in the cage for up to a weak before throwing them out . The lady who had spent so much time scowling at Diya died within the first month . They left her in the cage for 3 days after she passed . Her body became swollen and rigid , eyes glazed over . Diya could not stop from staring at the woman and was thankful when she was removed from the cage .

As the weeks turned into months Diya listened carefully to the whispers of other captives and the man running the boat talk . Diya learned that it was a slave ship heading to the New World . Slaves were worth a good price and worth the journey . It was really bad timing on Diya's part as they were just getting supplies from on land and came across her . Most of the people on board were from parts of Africa , a land a short journey from where Diya was . The captain was barely seen by any but was feared by all , including his men . Diya guess that these big burley men were Vikings . She had heard about these warriors from Ruth on their travels . Ruth would get wide eyed talking about the brutal men and how they always had safe ship routes for travel . Diya thinking back to this now realized Ruth had not been exaggerating but had only know the bare truth of the matter .

Diya was sure she died at least once or twice during the journey . She was thankful they did not clean out the cages everyday . She had become so sun blistered and dehydrated she was sure she had passed on many times during the journey . She would awake feeling refreshed and feeling somewhat guilty once looking around at everyone else . Death , sickness and greed surrounded her . This is what evil was .

Chapter 17

Day after day . Month after month .
Sun , rain , wind and water beat on Diya . She had
lost count of the days . For months she prayed to
god , every minute , every day . Begging him to let
her die as she watched others beside her pass
away . Just when she thought she could cry no
more the tears would start again fresh as the first
day . Diya woke up that morning and started to
pray when she heard a bird call . She stopped
praying and looked up to the sky . There was a
white bird flying above . Diya broke out in a huge
smile , a bird meant that land was near by . As if
on cue the men on the ship started cheering and
yelling land .

Within hours the ship had docked
and the cages were being opened . Men roughly

grabbed people from the cages and started lining them up , chaining them together with a rope . Diya crawled out quickly and got in line . She was surprised at how hard it was to stand up straight after sitting curled up for months . Taking a huge breath of air she forced herself to stand tall .

They were led off the boat , down the dock and onto a gravel road . Diya blinked her eyes in surprise . A vast village was before her . They walked down the road and around a couple corners before coming to a large courtyard . The man leading the group suddenly started yelling .

" Slaves for sale ! "

Diya cringed at the word slave . The man kept yelling and walking around the courtyard . People stopped and stared as the lineup walked by . It was as if they were cattle for sale . Men walked up and looked closer at some of the others in the line up . Diya jumped as she realized a man was standing beside her and had grabbed her ass !

" How much for this one ? " asked the man beside Diya pointing to her . She frowned and kept her head down .

" Come talk sir " said the man his voice still strong after so much yelling . The man beside Diya walked over . The men went in deep discussion and at times would point to people in the line up , including Diya . They eventually came to a agreement and shook hands to seal the deal . The man who had grabbed Diya's ass walked back over to Diya , he smiled at her and whispered in her ear .

" Your ass is mine now "

Diya shivered in disgust and was thankful as he walked away .

" Take them to holding " said the man who had been leading the line up , pointing at Diya and some others . A man came out of the crowd and collected everyone including Diya . They followed him for a short while before coming to a building . He opened the door and hurried them in .

Inside was a huge cell . Diya was surprised to see how large it was and how many people were crammed in it . She guessed that she had been bought by the creepy man and would wait here until he would pay and collect her .

" Hello ? " said a young woman's voice . Diya looked around trying to figure out where it had come from . Most of the people that had been on the ship with Diya barely spoke so she was surprised to hear a distinct hello . The gate opened again and more people were shoved into the cell . Diya looked around but could not hear anyone anymore . She found a corner and leaned against the wall exhausted .

Diya awoke to the voice again . She opened her eyes trying to pin point who it was coming from . It was dark and took a minute for her eyes to adjust .

" Hello ? " said Diya quietly into the darkness . Shuffling could be heard and then Diya felt someone tapping her on her shoulder .

" Hi ! " whispered a young girl standing beside her .

" Hi ? " answered Diya .

" You speak ! Can you help me ? " asked the young girl . She looked around the cell and then back at Diya .

" Help you ? " said Diya in confusion .

" Yes " replied the girl slowly as she leaned in to look at Diya .

" Do you understand me ? " asked the girl with concern .

" Yes " answered Diya .

" Oh gosh I thought you were just copying me like a simpleton " said the girl smiling .

Before Diya could say anything the girl grabbed her hand and started pulling her along the cell wall . She suddenly stopped letting go of Diya's hand . She bent over and started to feel the wall with her hands and pulled out a brick . Diya's eyes widened with surprise and she looked around

In fear someone else had seen , but everyone seemed to be sleeping .

" Boost me up " whispered the girl as she put her foot in the hole the brick had come from . Diya pushed the girl up against the wall , she grabbed the top of the wall and swung her feet over . Diya stood speechless staring at the girl .

" Give me your hands " whispered the girl as she held her hands out for Diya to grab . Taking one last look around the room it was not a hard decision for Diya . She put her foot in the hole and reached up grabbing the girls hands . Before she knew it Diya was on top of the cell wall staring down into the cell . She felt a tug on her foot and blindly dropped down on the other side .

" Follow me and keep down " whispered the girl as she creeped along the outside wall .

Diya followed the girl and did as she asked . The young girl was graceful and seemed to know where every guard was posted . It did not

take long before they were walking down a dark
alley .

" What is your name ? " whispered
Diya breaking the silence of the night .

" Billy " answered the girl .

" Billy ? " said Diya not sure if she
had heard right .

" Yes . My name was Bertha . What
a horrible name. I changed it to Billy . What is your
name ? " asked the young girl .

" Diya " answered Diya .

" Your pretty Diya " said Billy

" Thank you " said Diya again
surprised by this young girl .

They walked in silence for a hour or
so before Diya broke the silence again .

" How did you know how to
escape ? " asked Diya now curious .

" I have been there before "
answered Billy .

" I don't understand " said Diya .

Billy stopped walking and turned to look up at Diya .

" My brother takes me to market and sells me as a slave . When I get to the holding cell I wait until dark and get someone to give me a boost out . We live a couple hours away from here " explained Billy as she studied Diya's reaction .

" Why would your brother do that ? " asked Diya even more confused now .

" We need the money to live . " answered Billy as she started walking down the gravel road again .

" Oh " said Diya .

" My brother is not going to be happy " said Billy sadly .

" Why ? " asked Diya .

" You " answered Billy .

" What about me ? " asked Diya .

" I am not supposed to bring anyone home " answered Billy .

" Oh I see " said Diya now worried .

Here she was in a new land following a young girl in the night . Diya had no idea where she was or where to go . She needed Billy's help .

" Why did you help me ? " asked Diya .

" That man who bought you , he is a gross pervert " answered Billy with disgust . She kicked a rock off the path .

" Oh " said Diya .

" Then you helped me with no questions . I looked down at you and I just couldn't leave you to go home with that pig " said Billy in a matter of fact tone .

" Thank you " said Diya . She believed Billy and was truly thankful .

" Your welcome " said Billy .

" Are you sure it is ok I am with you ? " asked Diya nervously . She wanted to stay with Billy but did not want to go somewhere she would not be welcomed .

" He will get over it " answered Billy .

" You are a angel " whispered Diya .

They walked for hours . Diya enjoyed being able to stretch her legs for the first time in months .

Chapter 18

Billy and her brother Robert lived far out in the countryside . Diya learned that she had landed in somewhere called Boston . It was a hub point for all sea and land people to meet and trade . Billy and her brother had been stolen from their home as slaves to be sold , both barely living through the voyage across the seas. They were sold before they had even left the ship . Taken to the holding area , it did not take long for them to escape .

Living in the new world was challenging .Everything was different . They managed to find a quiet corner hours away from everyone else and adapt to their new life . Within years a small village had grown around them .

All people were escaped slaves , lost souls and misfits . Everyone coming together for one common reason , freedom .

Diya fit in perfectly . Robert at first upset with Billy for bringing home yet another mouth to feed soon learned that Diya could fend for herself . Diya was already a master at setting traps and soon was bringing back enough for all to eat . She showed Billy how to make a garden while Billy taught her about the local wildlife and landscape . There sat a empty chapel on the edge of the village. The last pastor , drunk one night , decided to have a gun fight with a local and lost . His cross stood alone beside the humble chapel . Diya feeling brave one day approached Robert .

" I am going to move into the chapel " said Diya firmly .

" What ? No hello ? " said Robert .

" Hi ! Sorry I did not mean to be rude " said Diya .

" I am just teasing Diya . You can

not move into the chapel , we are waiting for another pastor to join us then it will be his home . " said Robert .

"I will be the pastor " said Diya .

"You are a woman " said Robert .

"What does that have to do with it ? " asked Diya .

Robert paused to study Diya .

"Well ? " asked Diya impatiently .

"Fine " answered Robert .

"I can ? " asked Diya now excited .

"Yes . Go ahead . " answered Robert smiling . Diya jumped in joy and gave him a big hug .

"Thank you ! " said Diya as she collected what few belongings she had to move into the chapel .

Diya spent a week cleaning the chapel and arranging the seats for Sunday . The little church was perfect with a little room off the back for Diya . To her surprise it came with a bookshelf full of books , old bibles , music books , a wide selection . Some Diya had seen before and others were totally new to her eyes . Sunday came and to her surprise the chapel filled right up . She silently approached the front of the chapel to face her audience .

" Welcome all " said Diya loudly .

Some people nodded in response while others sat quietly . Diya caught her breath and looked over to see Billy sitting at the back , she was giving Diya thumbs up . Diya smiled .

" Today we rise above our past .It is read in Galatians 5:1 . It is for freedom that Christ has set us free . Stand firm , then , and do not let yourselves be burdened again by a yoke of slavery ! " said Diya loudly .

The chapel remained quiet as she studied the peoples faces looking for any response .

" AMEN ! " said a man as he stood up and started clapping . The people in the church joined in on the clapping with cheers of joy .

The rest of the sermon went by as if Diya had been preaching for years . Once done , person after person thanked Diya for the wonderful morning . She beamed with joy .

" You did really good Diya " said Billy as she walked up .

" Thank you " said Diya .

" Very surprising " said Robert walking up to stand beside Billy .

" How so ? " asked Diya .

" You are a breath of fresh air Diya " said Robert . His girlfriend shot him a dirty look and grabbed his hand to lead him out of the church .

" She is jealous of everything " said Billy watching her brother and his girlfriend walk away . Diya nodded in agreement .

Out of all the lives that Diya had lived she loved this one the most . It was freedom . She felt like it was her purpose to be in this strange land and preach gods word . Every Sunday without fail she would fill the church and give that weeks sermon . People started hearing about her and would travel hours just to hear Diya speak . Before she knew it , Diya was being asked to baptise children just born . During the week, people started showing up asking to speak to Diya for advice . She was always willing to help the best she could . It was a strange land with strange people a long way from home . Diya had never felt so much love from so many until now . She was blessed .

Outside the chapel , beside the pastors cross was a tall tree with weeping branches that would hang low , like a curtain to hide underneath . A stone bench sat as if it had been there for a eternity . It was smooth and chiseled . Diya would spend her evenings sitting on the bench , reading or preparing her next weeks sermon . She would listen to the soft sounds of the village and the people , it was comforting to her . One evening Diya heard a sound she had not heard for years . A melody being whistled . She almost dropped her book in surprise . Looking around she could not see where the sound was coming from .

Diya knew the tune well and whistled it back , looking all around for her long lost friends . The leaves started to rustle and before Diya knew it a hundred Floras were circling her in joy . She dropped the book and started to laugh . Her old friend stopped in front of her face .

" Hi " said the Flora .

Diya spent the evening catching up with her long lost friends . Again when she questioned where they had been , the subject would be changed . The Floras however remained unchanged , not one had aged a day , just like Diya . Conversation skills had grown a little but not much . Mostly Diya would watch them fly and play , thankful to see them again . The Floras were like a part of home for Diya . She cherished them . Just as fast as they had show up they left even faster . Billy came walking down the path .

" Diya ? " asked Billy .

" Yes ? " answered Diya quietly as she looked for any sign of the Floras .

" Are you alright ? " asked Billy with concern .

" Yes of course " answered Diya promptly . She was not alright . She wondered where the Floras had went and what they did when she did not see them for long periods of time . Perhaps they knew another like her she hoped .

" You don't seem ok " said Billy looking closely at Diya .

" Just missing old friends " said Diya truthfully as she looked up at the sky .

" I get that " said Billy with sadness in her voice .

" What are you up to ? " asked Diya changing the subject .

" Oh , yes ! " said Billy suddenly remembering . She paused and then continued .

" There are rumours of slave hunters near by " said Billy as she frowned .

" Slave hunters ? " said Diya shocked .

" Yes , they are paid to collect run away slaves . Dead or alive " explained Billy .

" That's not good " said Diya worried now .

" It is just a rumour , they never come this far in the country . I am sure we will all be fine , but if you see anyone out of the ordinary please let Robert know ." said Billy in a very serious tone .

" Of course ! " said Diya now deep in thought . She had never heard of these slave hunters before today .

" It will be ok " said Billy .

" Thank you for everything Billy . I have never been happier then I have been here . I know it has only been a couple years but you all truly feel like family to me " said Diya bashfully .

" Diya ! You are our family now and we are never going to give you up ! " said Billy.

Diya gave Billy a big hug before she went on her way to spread the news of the slave hunters to the other villagers . Diya gave a whistle but the Floras were long gone . She stood , with hands on hips , puzzled by the Floras and perplexed by the mention of slave hunters .

Diya got down on her knees and put her hands together .

" Lord please give me a sign that I belong here , doing your work . Amen "

Chapter 19

Diya woke up to hot flames blistering her skin . She gasped for air and inhaled thick black smoke . In the distance she could hear screaming , like someone was in pain . She tried to stand up and fell to the floor . The flames kept biting at her skin and then everything went black .

Smoke . Diya woke up to the smell of smoke . This seemed so familiar . Diya opened her eyes and could see she lay in a bed of ash. Above her was blue sky with burnt branches on the tree . There was no chapel anymore . Diya's mouth opened in amazement but no noise came out . Tears started running down her face as she slowly got up from the rubble and stood up . Bewildered at first Diya brushed herself off trying to figure out what happened . Diya carefully made her way out of the burnt chapel when she realized there was smoke in the sky ahead of her , the village ! She broke into a run . Rounding the corner she stopped in her tracks . Bodies were hanging from the trees . Diya screamed in surprise . The village was gone . All the buildings were now little piles of ash , some still had embers glowing bright . Diya turned in horror to come face to face with Billy hanging in a tree . Her eyes glossed over , swinging back and forth as if she might still be alive . Diya fell to the ground sobbing .

" WHY ?? " screamed Diya looking up at the sky .

Silence . Not even a rustle of the leaves . Just the smell of death and smoke .

" I HAVE DONE EVERYTHING YOU WANTED !! WHY DO YOU PUNISH ME ? " screamed Diya still looking up at the sky .

" WE HAVE A LIVE ONE OVER HERE ! " yelled a mans voice in the distance .

Diya was crying so hard that she did not hear the man yelling . She lay on the ground sobbing .

" Get up " said a mans voice suddenly .

Diya surprised stopped crying and opened her eyes . A tall man stood before her .

" GET UP ! " the man repeated himself this time yelling at Diya .

Diya slowly got up from the ground and stood in front of the man .

" You stupid slave bitch , probably to stupid to understand me . " said the man looking at Diya with disgust .

Diya looked the man in the eye and spit right on his face . Before she knew it he wound up and punched her in the face . She fell to the ground unconscious .

Diya woke up not sure of how long she had been unconscious for , her jaw was throbbing with pain . The man who had punched her was now standing with another man talking .

Diya slowly started to crawl away trying to keep low to the ground and as quiet as she could .

" HEY ! " exclaimed one of the men .

Diya burst to her feet and started to run as fast as she could . She could hear the two men close behind her . She was sure these were the slave hunters that Billy had talked about , killing all escaped slaves as they were deemed traitors of the land . Diya weaved in and out of the trees easily losing the two men . She could hear them in the distance yelling for her . Diya tried to whistle for the Floras help , but not a one appeared .

" Where you looking for me ? " whispered a mans voice .

Diya screamed and started to run but was quickly caught in some rope and fell to the ground with a hard thud . Looking up she could see a man on a horse holding the rope , he gave the rope a tug and then gave the horse a kick . The horse surprised by all the action stood up on its hind legs and threw the man off . The man landed next to Diya , his head hitting a rock , blood started pouring from the wound . The horse satisfied stood there assessing the situation not moving . Diya quickly untied herself from the rope and stood up , the man remained unmoving on the ground . Diya walked over to the horse as if they were long lost friends , she rubbed his head and he lowered it for her . She grabbed his neck and boosted herself up on the horse . Diya was surprised , the horse stayed calm as if this was nothing new .

Hearing the men in the distance , she gave the horse a gentle nudge and headed off in the opposite direction . The horse obeyed and started a gentle run . Diya rode for hours before setting up camp by a little stream . She had one more good cry to mourn the loss of her friend Billy and the village she had grown so found of . Diya made a little fire and curled herself around it . She couldn't sleep and just stared at the flame as it jumped and crackled with the breeze .

Diya dreamt that night . She could not remember the last time she had dreamt . It was bits and pieces of her long life all jumbled together , every moment consumed by fire . Then she was somewhere new with creatures she had never seen . Diya was not scared but somehow felt safe in all the chaos . She woke up in a sweat , the morning light shone brightly as if offering unseen hope . She wondered what her dream meant if anything . The horse bent over and nudged Diya's shoulder as if saying it was time to go . Diya reached up and gave the horse a quick pet .

Diya rode the horse for 3 days before reaching the port called Boston . Here she was less then two years back where she had started . It did not take long to sell the horse , which gave her enough money to rent a room for the month . She had enough left over to buy a much needed bath and something to eat . The town was the largest Diya had ever seen . Buildings loomed over the simple streets with oil lights to

light the streets at night . There were vendors
everywhere , offering up whatever they had . Some
played music with a cup for any money that could
be spared .

Diya would explore the city called
Boston everyday . On the third day she found a
church . It was a grand building with beautiful
stained glass for each window . The pastor was a
joyous man who welcomed Diya in for prayer .

" Are you from here ? " asked the
pastor .

" No . I come from another land . "
answered Diya cautiously .

" What brought you to the church ?
" asked the pastor changing the subject .

" God " answered Diya smiling .

" Oh you're a smart one " said the
pastor chuckling .

" I don't know my purpose " said
Diya suddenly .

" What can you give to god ? " asked

the pastor .

" My everything of course "
answered Diya proudly .

" The lord has given us all our own
special talent to use while we are here . What do
you feel like your special talent is ? " asked the
pastor .

" What if a person is immortal ? Is
that a special talent ? " asked Diya .

" No one is immortal other then god
" answered the pastor somewhat annoyed .

" But what if ? " asked Diya .

" They would be a abomination "
answered the pastor .

" But god makes all in his
likeness , so how would that person be a
abomination ? " asked Diya .

" Do you know of such a person ? "
asked the pastor with a serious tone watching Diya
as she answered .

" No " answered Diya quickly .

The pastor paced around the room perplexed .

" This is a very strange conversation " said the pastor as he sat down across from Diya .

" I have a active imagination I am sorry " explained Diya smiling at the pastor .

" How would such a person earn gods grace ? " asked Diya .

" If such a person were to exist and wanted grace from god ... " said the pastor looking deep in thought trying to chose his words carefully . Diya sat forward in her seat hoping the pastor would tell her something unknown .

" Faith " said the pastor suddenly with excitement .

" Faith ? " asked Diya confused .

Diya was surprised by the pastors answer and angered by it at the same time . She had spent her life having nothing but faith in god . She had devoted her every thought to god and he had ignored her .

" If a person is immortal , they must have faith that god has a plan for them . The journey is preparing the person for their destiny . Even if that person is a abomination in our standards , god made them for a reason I believe . " answered the pastor looking satisfied with his conclusion .

" I see " said Diya not satisfied with his answer .

" Now you have to let this all go . It is ridiculous talk for a girl your age " said the pastor .

Diya almost burst out laughing , if only he knew how what her age was and how right he was that she had to let it go and have faith .

Chapter 20

It was the 1800's and Boston was booming . Thousands of people lived in the city , many strangers from other lands . Diya learned quickly how to survive city life . It was easy to blend into the busy hustle of the streets . She loved the street merchants as they were often the kindest to her . Diya found many jobs over the years to keep her fed with her own room . She spent a lot of time working in wash houses until her hands were cracked and bleeding , cleaning houses and doing errands for the wealthy . Diya did not mind the hard work , it made the days pass quickly and gave her a feeling of accomplishment .

The church remained in Diya's life . She would attend services everyday . The pastors

advice to let it go started to make sense to Diya .
She had spent most of her life angry at god for not
letting her die , instead she should have been
rejoicing at his wonderful gift to her . Let it go she
would repeat to herself . Diya realized that at this
point she was well over a thousand years old and
still had lessons to learn .

   Years past by and the city grew with
every breath Diya took . It was really quite
amazing she thought . She became apart of it , like
a ghost in the background ever present . At one
point she took a job in the brothel district . One of
the madams needed a helper , to answer the door ,
take appointments and be her eyes when she was
not present . At first Diya was insulted by the job
offer , and then scolded herself wondering why she
would feel that way . She took the job against her
own judgement as if she was trying to prove
something to herself , and she did . Diya fell in love
with the brothel life . She could never be one of the
ladies who welcomed men but she very quickly

grew to admire and respect them . They were all very hard working ladies , many educated such as Diya . This shocked Diya as she had already made up her mind about such ladies and here she was wrong . Most were smart , enterprising women who wanted a better life if not a different future . It was bittersweet as often the ladies would come out with a black eye or even worse beat up . They would take many medicines to help with many ailments sometimes resulting in death . Diya was thankful that her body was hers and only hers . She worked there until a sickness passed through the brothel district , killing over half of the people , including her .

There was a dumping grounds outside of the city that Diya knew well . She had awoken in the same field throughout the hundreds of years she lived in Boston . When servants or workers would die and not be claimed they would end up thrown in the field . They commoners had given it a name , amissa animabus which translated from latin to english as lost souls . At times Diya would come back to life breathing in air to be face to face with a co worker still dead , crows picking at their skin . It was a reminder of how futile and short life could be for some . She would say a prayer for the dead and then give thanks for her ever lasting life .

A lot of time was spent upon a hill top watching the ships come in and out of dock . At times Diya missed the sea life but had grown found of Boston to much so to leave it . It had grown on her as the years passed by without notice . Diya felt as if she was growing with the town , the new roads , the buildings that seemed to go to the heavens . She knew every road and alley. Boston felt like home .

A sickness came in one day on one of the ships and slowly spread throughout the town . It was nothing like Diya had ever seen before . The little shops started opening , right by the brothels . They sold what they called a miracle , a escape or even a meeting with god . So many promises of this new thing called opium . So easy just light the pipe and inhale , all your worries go away for just a small price . Diya called it a sickness because of what it did and how it spread without anyone knowing . She knew first hand and it had horrified her . Diya had tried the black smoke looking for her answer and ended up lost in confusion for months . Once she had tasted the smoke she could not stop , even though it gave her no answers and took everything she owned , including her soul . The monster had stolen her and it did not stop until it had taken everything from her including her life . When she awoke that day , in the field of lost souls , it was different . Diya cried , almost a howl like a wounded animal . A cart with men was still there , unloading bodies . Seeing her sit up , gasp for breath and then cry a unearthly howl sent the men running in fear . This time of all the times Diya had died , she was the most thankful to be back , more thankful to be out of the fog that had consumed her life .

Diya never went back to that part of city . She found a orphanage to work at , they eagerly accepted her help and gave her a home . Diya enjoyed the children , loving each as her own . She would do everything as a mother would for the children , giving out hugs freely . The nuns who ran it called her the light , as she would brighten up any room she walked into . She never told the nuns it was what her name meant in essence . Her favorite part was reading books for the children . She would do different voices , making the stories come alive . Diya wished , just once she could stay with these nuns and lost children , forever . But she knew all to well that nothing lasted forever . Diya learned to cherish every moment before it was gone and she had to relearn a whole new reality . She would pray that god now let her have one life not a million different lives . She did not want to die anymore , Diya just wanted the same reality . She knew it was a fleeting dream but would still pray for it daily .

Diya would call for the Floras
anytime she could make it outside of the city . She
would whistle and wait patiently , but no Flora
would ever come . Diya would be sad as she did not
want to lose her memory of her friends as time
seemed to go slow but so fast at the same time .

Suitors would come and go over
time . Sometimes Diya would agree to go out on a
date or socialize . No one compared to her one true
love Darius . Even though hundreds of years had
already passed by her heart still ached for him . At
times she would fool herself thinking she would see
him , walking down a road or on a ship . She
would run with excitement and then realize it was
not him at all . It was not just Darius that she
would fool herself into seeing , it was many people
she had known and loved during her long life . It
would sadden her suddenly , remembering a friend
that she had not thought about for sometimes
hundreds of years . Besides for the fact of missing

Darius , Diya just felt like it was to hard . It was easy to fall in love , it was hard to keep up the lies . Why she was not aging , why she had no family and then to disappear one day . It was worth more effort then the joy she received in return . Diya was blessed to have found one true love in her life , no one could or ever would compare to what her and Darius had .

So the orphanage would do for now . There she had unconditional pure love from the children . At least until her time had run out . Which ironically was only a week later . It was a fluke accident , Diya did not see it coming . It was a beautiful day , blue skies with not a cloud in the sky . She had gathered all the children in the field next to the orphanage , wild flowers blew in the breeze like a silent musical . They had started a game of tag , everyone running around in circles . The children were having so much fun with smiles so big . Then it all ended . A arrow came out of no where and pierced Diya in the heart .

212

It all seemed surreal to Diya . She looked down and saw the arrow sticking out of her chest , then looked up at the smiling children and then fell to the ground and darkness . The orphanage put on a beautiful funeral for Diya . The first that had ever been done for her in her long life . She had woken up in a coffin in the basement of the orphanage and snuck out . Diya asked around and found out that it had been a random arrow from hunters near by . A fluke accident .

A loneliness overcome Diya . She had not been prepared to leave the orphanage so quickly. Diya as always had to move to another area of town in fear of being recognized . She walked for over a hour and found a butcher house , walking in she started inquiring about a job when she heard her name being called . Diya froze . Who would be calling her ?

" Diya ? " asked a older lady as she walked up to Diya .

" Excuse me ? " answered Diya as

213

she turned to face the lady .

        " Are you Diya ? " asked the lady moving closer to look .

        " No sorry " answered Diya as she studied the lady . Then she realized it was sister Grace from the orphanage . She gasped and stepped back .

        " Sorry . You look identical to a lady who just passed away I knew . Do you have a sister or cousin named Diya ? Such a sweet sweet lady she was " said Sister Grace .

        It was that moment that Diya knew she had to leave her sweet city called Boston .

Chapter 21

Diya heard the city whisper in her ear later that evening as she walk through the market . New York . At first she was startled , looking to see who had whispered in her ear , but could see no one near her . Again she heard the raspy voice whispering , New York . Diya had heard of the great city and all of its wonders . Was her mind playing tricks with her or was this god trying to give her a sign . She continued wandering through the market not sure of what or who she was looking for . Diya stopped at a fruit stand , hungry , not sure of how long it had been since she had eaten . The lady running it looked Diya up and down and offered her a apple .

" I do not have anything to offer "

explained Diya sadly .

" No charge my darling " replied the lady with a warm smile .

" Thank you " said Diya with as much warmth as she could muster .

" You know that apple came all the way from New York " said the lady and then she turned to help another customer .

Diya smiled at the lady , bowed and left . She knew now that she must go to New York and there was only one way to get there . Train . As brave as Diya was , she knew there was no way she could make the journey to New York on foot . The wildlife and the villages along the way were unknown to her . She had heard stories of bears and cougars eating people in their sleep . Worse yet she had heard tales of villages scalping people who happen into their property . None of this Diya wished to experience .

The train ride to the great city was over 7 days long with many stops . Diya had no money and nothing to sell . She did not want to acquire another job in Boston but rather leave right away . Sneaking onto the train station property one night she snuck into a cargo car near the back of the train . Diya squeezed herself in between boxes , making herself a little spot concealed from prying eyes .

The train left the next morning . It was loud , unkind to her ears . Diya had a sack of water and a pocket full of dry bread . It was going to be a long journey , but it was on her terms , so somehow that made everything easier . The first day was easy as she slept for most of the journey . Diya awoke when the train came to a stop as the boxes and crates around her shook . She listened carefully and sat still hoping not to be found . But no one came and opening the cargo car . The next couple days went by fairly fast . Diya spent most of her time watching the countryside through the cracks in the train cars wall . This country was much bigger then she had expected , so wild and untouched it seemed .

On the fourth day , before the train left that morning . The cargo door opened . Diya caught off guard did her best to hide among the boxes . Some workers came in and started moving cargo out . One of the workers walked to the back of the car and made eye contact with Diya . She froze , unsure of what to do . He simply shook his head and turned away , telling the other workers they had gotten everything that they were sent for . As the train car door closed , Diya let out a sigh of relief .

Before Diya knew it , 7 days had past and they were pulling into the city . Her eyes widened as she watched the buildings get bigger and bigger . So many people , dressed so nice . It was overwhelming . The train came to a abrupt stop and Diya could hear the conductor announce the arrival at New York train station . Standing up she brushed herself off cautiously opening the cargo door to peak out . It was a chaos of people .

Diya took her chance , opening the door and jumping out . She followed the crowd as it made its way out of the train station as if they were a group of animals , being herded out to pasture . As they grew further away from the station the crowd silently disappeared in different directions leaving Diya alone . She pondered at which way to go when she heard a bird call . Looking up she saw pigeons fly overhead and decided to follow their direction . It was as if the heavens had opened up and Diya was following all the signals . Everything had been going so smoothly Diya thought to herself as she walked down the path beside the roadway . The houses grew into buildings and soon Diya found herself in the heart of the city . Looking up she saw the church off in the distance and smiled , this must be her destiny .

The day had quickly turned into night as Diya walked towards the church . The city was a buzz of noise with shots of laughter often filling the air . The church now seemed like a beacon in the night , with its stained glass windows glowing from the full moon light . With relief Diya finally reached its big wooden doors , she was exhausted from the day . Reaching up she tried to open the door but it was locked . Confused at first as Diya had never found the door to a church locked before , she took a step back and decided to knock . It must be some mistake she thought to herself as the church was always open for all . Diya knocked on the door and waited , nothing happened . She knocked again , this time louder , but not a sound from the church . Looking around Diya could see no one , raising her fist to knock again she heard a noise and realized it was a small hole in the door had opened .

" Hello ? " said Diya .

" Go away ! " said a mans voice from behind the door .

" Excuse me ? " said Diya surprised .

" GO AWAY ! " yelled the man .

" I think you have me confused with someone else sir " said Diya .

" No I do not . Go away before I call the authorities and have you REMOVED ! GO ! " said the voice behind the door angerly .

" But ... " said Diya confused . What was happening ? She did not understand .

" Go ! Get out of here ! GO ! " yelled the man .

Diya backed away from the church door and made her way down the stairs like a wounded animal . She heard the little window slot in the door shut . Looking back up at the church she wondered what just had happened . Deciding that it was late and obviously there had been some mix up , Diya found a spot under neath a tree by the church . She was confident that morning would bring better results and clarity to the situation . But it did not . When morning came , she awoke with a smile and headed right back up the stairs to the church doors . They were still locked . She frowned . Again she knocked several times before the same angry mans voice yelled at her to go away again .

Bewildered Diya sat down on the church steps deciding on what to do . She had been sure that this was were she was supposed to be , but yet was being told to go away . Then she heard the church door start to open . Diya ran up the stairs to face whoever was opening the door . The door opened and before she knew it , a pail of dirty water was thrown in her face . The church door slammed and she again heard the mans voice yell at her to go away . Diya was stunned and just stood there for a minute trying to grasp at what had just happened . She could not believe this was happening . Where was she supposed to go ?

Diya took one last look at the church and started down the road . It was clear she was un welcome there , for what reason she did not know and tried not to take it personally . Diya wandered for hours throughout the city . It was grand in size and she was lost within the first hour . She started asking for work and people directed her to the street markets saying she might find luck there .

Diya felt like she did not belong in this big city . She was taller then most women , darker with her deep blue eyes . Not so many people had any markings on their skin which made her painfully more aware of hers . As she wandered she wondered why she felt like this , maybe it was the rejection by the church , maybe it was her sense of being completely lost in this new city .

The market was crowded with vendors . Diya surprised at the size of it , block after block , everything you could think of for sale . It seemed never ending , you would turn a corner and there would be more . Diya's mouth watered as all the food smells wafted past her nose . Some she recognized and others unknown . Her stomach growled at the sudden hunger . She had to figure out someway to eat , to live here .

Then she heard a voice that she had not heard for over a thousand years .

" Saphire ? " whispered Diya .

Chapter 22

Diya followed the voice down the alley and came face to face with Saphire . She was dressed in a fancy robe with her hair all dressed with jewels , looking the same as the last day Diya had seen her . Looking right past Diya , Saphire called out to the crowd .

" Let me tell you your future " yelled Saphire to the crowd .

A lady walked up and handed Saphire some change . She sat down at a small table . Saphire took her hand and looked deeply into it . Diya watched , not believing that this could be her friend from so long ago . Saphire leaned forward and whispered into the ladies ear . The lady smiled and thanked Saphire , leaving quickly to tell her news to her friends . Saphire sat back looking smug as a cat .

Diya quickly sat down at the table . Saphire not looking up grabbed Diya's hand .

" Do you have a question ? " asked Saphire as she opened Diya's palm to read . Diya relaxed her hand , watching intently . Saphire froze suddenly and slowly looked up at Diya .

" Saphire ? " whispered Diya as Saphire made eye contact . Saphire dropped Diya's hand as if it had burned her .

" Diya ? " asked Saphire in utter shock and surprise .

Diya nodded her head yes . Saphire jumped up and wrapped her arms around Diya , hugging her tight . Then just as suddenly she let go and stepped back to study Diya .

" Did he send you ? " asked Saphire .

" Did who send me ? " answered Diya puzzled .

" Oh he is good . You almost had me ! " said Saphire crossing her arms still looking Diya up and down .

" How are you alive ? " asked Diya .

" Same way you are alive or at least seem to be " answered Saphire impatiently .

" You can not die either ? " asked Diya hopefully .

" What ? You already died I know that . This is some sick joke that master likes to play , I know it . " said Saphire looking around at the people surrounding them .

" Yes it is true I have died , but I never stay dead . I am always reborn " explained Diya .

" Seriously ? " said Saphire looking Diya in her eyes .

" Yes , seriously . " said Diya staring right back into Saphires eyes .

" That is not possible " said Saphire .

" Yet here I stand before you , how else do you explain that ? " said Diya firmly .

" You made a deal with master " said Saphire .

" Who is master ? " asked Diya .

" Lucifer !? " exclaimed Saphire .

Diya gasped with surprise and took a step back .

" That's not possible !! " exclaimed Diya looking at Saphire in horror .

" And yet , here I stand " said Saphire firmly .

The two just stood in the busy market staring at each other . The world seemed to stop for a minute and all the sounds of the market disappeared in the distance as if they had been placed in the middle of a whirlwind storm . Saphire raised her hand to Diya and Diya eagerly grabbed it . Lighting bolts hit the ground around them and shook the ground . Diya's eyes wide with amazement watched as Saphire seemed to glow , her blond hair taking on a life of its own . Diya did not know if they were there for minutes or hours , Saphire let go of Diya's hand . The whirlwind and lighting were gone as fast as they had come . The market noise came crashing back like a wave hitting Diya in the face . She grabbed the table to re adjust and looked up at Saphire who was smiling from ear to ear .

" I have missed you my friend " said Saphire .

" I have missed you as well " said Diya .

" You are different " said Saphire .

" So are you . Did you really make a deal with the devil ? " asked Diya .

" Yes " answered Saphire as she looked around the crowd .

" Why ? " asked Diya .

" It is a good gig " answered Saphire laughing at her own humour .

" Ha ha . Seriously Saphire . The

Devil ? " said Diya with concern .

" It is not as bad as it sounds Diya . I wanted to stay young and beautiful " Saphire paused to look in a mirror before continuing on . " It has worked out very well for me , I think I got the better of the deal to be honest "

Diya scoffed and looked away .

" How has your god helped you ? " asked Saphire eyes darker then the night .

Diya thought back to the previous night . The man at the church door yelling at her to leave .

" He brought me to you " said Diya .

" Are you sure that was god ? " asked Saphire sincerely .

Diya looked at Saphire wide eyed unable to answer . She had never considered hell or the devil himself in the picture . Diya had always concentrated on god and his work . Yet here was Saphire standing before her , work of the devil .

" There must be some reason you

have not stayed dead . I know why I am alive . But you .... Even when I tried to read your existence it was shadowed from me " explained Saphire .

" What are you trying to say ? " asked Diya .

" Maybe you should come home with me " said Saphire .

" Home ? " asked Diya confused .

" Yes . It could be our home . Come with me . I have a huge castle . " answered Saphire with excitement in her eyes .

" In hell ? " asked Diya in shock .

" Well yes , it is really very nice . You would be treated very well I can promise you that . " said Saphire .

" I believe in god Saphire " said Diya defiantly .

" I am not telling you not to believe in god Diya . " said Saphire sarcastically .

The market place got even busier and a lady asked for a reading from Saphire .

" Just think about it Diya . There is some bread and water in the corner , have a seat and rest . You must be tired of running my friend " said Saphire . She turned to the lady and sat down to give her a reading .

Diya did as she was told and sat down in the corner , eating the bread and drinking the water . She watched as Saphire wowed person after person , mostly middle aged women looking for hope it seemed . Saphire was right , Diya was tired of running from every life she had . She would love to be in one place with a friend who understood her for who she was , but hell ? Was this gods plan for her ? Diya sat feeling full and safe watching all the activities of the market . Hours passed as Diya observed Saphire while she worked , she had forgotten how absolutely beautiful Saphire was . She was also very kind and soft with her words . It was hard to believe she had made a deal with the devil himself .

" Excuse me ? " said a man from

beside the tent . Diya jumped in surprise . She had

not seen him walk up . He had a cart and it was

full of books , Diya stared at the cart for a minute

surprised before looking back up at the man . He

was very handsome with very defined features .

Dark hair in waves around his pale face with dark

eyes .

" Are you alright ? " asked the man

with concern .

" Yes , thank you " answered Diya

as she looked again at the random cart of books .

" You like books ? " asked the man .

" Yes . I love to read . " answered

Diya feeling like a shy child suddenly . She looked

over and saw Saphire busy with another palm

reading . She caught her eye and Saphire gave her

a wink before turning her attention back to the

ladies waiting palm .

" Have you any experience in a

library ? " asked the man with a serious tone .

" Yes " answered Diya with joy .

" I am not bragging , but , I have one of the largest libraries in existence " said the man proudly .

" That is impressive " said Diya . She was not sure if the man was bragging or just proud .

" I am actually looking for someone to be in charge of it , run it so to speak " said the man as he looked at Diya .

" I have experience with libraries " blurted out Diya suddenly .

" Would you like the job ? " asked the man .

Diya looked at him surprised and then surprised herself with her answer .

" Yes "

Chapter 23

" So ? What did you think of him ? "
whispered Saphire into Diya's ear .

" Who ? " asked Diya . The man she
had been talking to had disappeared , cart and
all . With panic she looked around trying to pin
point where he had gone .

" Master " answered Saphire .

" I never saw him . I just got offered
a job at a library Saphire ! I said yes ! " said Diya
as she continued to scan the busy market looking
for the man .

" That was master silly " said
Saphire smiling .

" No " said Diya .

" Yes " said Saphire nodding her

head as if it would confirm her answer .

" But ... " Diya started to argue but stopped herself unsure now of what exactly the truth was .

" He is a nice guy . Not all horns and flames Diya . He offered you a job ? That means he likes you ! Pretty lucky ! " said Saphire gushing with joy . She started to pack up her belongings .

" I just took a job running the devils library ? " asked Diya in disbelief .

" Pretty cool , right ? I am done here . Lets go home , shall we ? " said Saphire .

" To hell ? " asked Diya .

" Yes Diya " answered Saphire .

Saphire started weaving her way through the people in the market . Diya followed closely , curious as to how one would get to hell . They rounded a corner and Diya could see the church's cross standing proud in the night sky , she gave a little prayer before continuing her unknown journey with her long lost friend .

They walked for a bit before coming to a short alley . Saphire walked up a brick wall and knocked three times , she stepped back and waited patiently . Diya watched as a part of the brick wall opened up as if it was a door . Saphire grabbed Diya's hand and walked through the brick doorway . The door shut behind them leaving them in total darkness . Diya held on to Saphire's hand tightly . Saphire confidently walked forward .

" Do not let go of my hand " whispered Saphire .

The darkness turned even darker and Diya swore she could hear crying in the distance . The air grew thick with heat . Diya did not know how long they walked , it could have been minutes or hours . Time did not seem to matter at that moment .

" We are here " said Saphire breaking the silence and letting go of Diya's hand .

It went from darkness to blinding

brightness . Diya rubbed her eyes as they slowly adjusted to the change . They were in a garden .

"This is beautiful " whispered Diya.

"Wait until you see our castle " said Saphire proudly .

Saphire had been right . The castle was more grand then anything Diya could have ever thought of . She had her own room , so big that when she spoke it echoed . A pool , always the perfect temperature with big colorful birds called peacocks wandering around . Diya spent her first week in hell just wandering around the castle .

A letter addressed to Diya showed up on the 7th day . The letter welcomed her to her new position at the library with her starting date included . It was signed Lucifer . She examined the letter and sighed . Never a day in her life did Diya think she would be working for the devil .

Saphire proved to be a great host . Taking Diya on trips around hell everyday to make her feel at home . If Diya did not know better she would have thought she was in heaven . Not one person Diya met had judgement towards her , they were all very welcoming . This caught her off guard . Even the demons were nothing like Diya had imagined , they would joke with her as if they were old friends . As much as Diya tried to dislike hell , she learned a new way to love it everyday .

The library was like nothing Diya had ever seen . It was a quick walk from the castle and was even more beautiful . Thousands of books lined the walls . A simple desk sat in the middle of the giant room with a single chair . Sitting down at the desk Diya realized she was surrounded by books , her dream come true . There was one thing Diya had not planned on and had taken her by such surprise that she almost fell over . She had shown up exactly as she was told to , entering the library she gasped at the size . Seeing the desk and no one around Diya sat down and closed her eyes . Within minutes she heard a sound she remembered from long ago , opening her eyes to her joy it was the Floras .

" Hi " said a group of Floras as they flew by Diya and continued up to the high ceiling until they looked like little dots .

" This is where you have been ? " yelled Diya to the room full of Floras . She got dizzy watching them fly round and round and sat back down at the desk . Diya had never been happier .

Time flew by fast for Diya . She had a excitement she had never felt before . Her mouth grew sore from smiling so much . The Floras were the perfect library assistants . As soon as she thought about a book , a Flora would appear and drop it on her desk . Apparently they had not worked well with past librarian's and at times had even tortured them . The fact that they had traveled so far to be with Diya throughout her life was unheard of , this made Diya feel special . She often wondered how they had found her in the first place but understood that some questions did not have any answers , some things were just meant to be .

Diya was thankful for the Floras

and to be re united with them at last . She spent

years reading every book she could find in hells

library . The Flora's became like her second hand ,

Diya learned to depend and more importantly trust

them .

Hell was infinite Diya soon learned .

Every week she would venture further into the

depths of hell . Diya was surprised that it did not

bother her , the torture , screaming and people

begging for there lives . They would not be there if

they had been good people , every person in hell ,

deserved to be in hell . Some people had come to

terms with who they were and took the punishment

assigned, while others acted as if it was a total

surprise to be in hell . The demons who gave out

such punishment treated it as a job , they took

pride in thier work and just wanted to please their

master . Really when it all came down to it , hell

ran rather smoothly . All and all Diya was

impressed .

Diya made friends, at first she refused any friendships . But as the years passed it was hard to ignore the same friendly faces . Diya enjoyed these friendships the most . She knew they would never grow old or die . Just like her . Hell slowly became home to Diya . She prayed everyday to god but he never answered . If Diya beckoned the devil , he showed up in minutes , with a smile on his face , inquiring how she was .

The library kept Diya busy . To her surprise lots of hells residents loved to read , including the devil himself . Diya became a personal confident to many as they dropped off books to take out new ones . One of her favorite people next to Saphire was a demon called Erika. She had come into the library one day all shy and timid . Erika was a beautiful red demon thought, taller then Diya with a long tail and long red hair . Her skin glowed a red so intense it looked like flames at times . Diya wondered what a demon could possibly want with a library .

242

" Can I help you ? " asked Diya .

" I guess " answered Erika looking around the library .

" Do you know what kind of book you want to read ? " asked Diya .

" Ok ... I would like books on ... " Erika paused and looked very uncomfortable .

" On ? " asked Diya gently .

" How to be human " said Erika in a rush sounding embarrassed .

" It is ok to be curious " said Diya hiding her surprise .

A Flora fly by dropping a book on Diya's desk . The title read " How to be human " . Both Diya and Erika stared at the book for a minute before Diya reached out and grabbed it off of the desk .

" It has pictures as well " said Diya .

" What does ? " asked Erika sharply.

" The book you have " replied Diya .

" Oh " said Erika .

" If your curious about humans I can tell you lots if you want to hang out sometime ? " asked Diya .

" Yes I would like that " said Erika with a smile .

A new friendship was made . A unlikely pair but the conversation never ran dry between the two . Both had curiosity , Diya about hell and Erika about being human .

Chapter 24

As more years passed on , Diya ,
Erika and Saphire became the best of friends .
Always spending any free time together . Diya loved
her new life . The three of them would spend
evenings exploring hell , having great discussions
of how to improve hell or Diya's favorite , playing a
game called cards . They were a unlikely trio it
seemed at first . Diya being the brains , Saphire
the looks and Erika the brawn . Each
complimented each other , which made for the
most interesting conversations between them.

Diya was lost in a book when the
library door swung open and in walked Erika all
full of life .

" Good morning beautiful or is it

afternoon ? I lose track of time in here " said Diya

pausing her reading to look up at Erika . The

Flora's flew down and started circling around her .

She started swinging her hands and tail trying to

shoo them away . It made Diya laugh , it was a

comical sight . A tall red fiery demon cursing at the

cutest white furry flying creatures . Erika would

always complain about the Flora's , saying they

were evil little pests made from the mud of hell .

She would never go into detail why she had so

much distaste for Diya's beloved Flora's .

" I have to be a babysitter ! " said

Erika pouting as she approached Diya .

" A babysitter ? " asked Diya .

" Master brought a living down here

to marry and I have to babysit her " explained

Erika .

" He is getting married ? What is a

living ? He can do that ? " asked Diya full of

questions now . She had never heard of the devil

getting married , or had even thought of him

wanting to be married until now .

" Oh ya , the devil gets out there . "
replied Erika .

" Why ? Does he get lonely ? " asked
Diya still confused . She just didn't think of the
devil as the dating / marriage type .

" He is trying for his 6th son silly "
answered Erika looking at Diya like she was daft .

" He has kids ? " asked Diya
surprised .

" Where have you been Diya ? Of
course he has kids . I think he has like over 20
daughters and 5 sons . " answered Erika .

Diya looked at Erika annoyed .
Sometimes it was like talking to a child when Erika
was in one of her moods .

" Why does he want a 6th son ?
Doesn't he have enough kids now ? " asked Diya .

Erika rolled her eyes at Diya's
question . Diya sat patiently waiting for the
answer .

" I swear Diya , your so smart but so dumb at times . How have you not heard about the 6th son ? " said Erika .

" I don't know ? " said Diya .

" If master has a 6th son then it opens up a whole new level of terror . Upperworld and everything we know about the living will be gone . " explained Erika with a serious tone .

" Oh " said Diya . She was unaware of this and was surprised she had not read anything in all her life that had even mentioned the 6th son .

" Ya kind of a big deal . He has been trying for hundreds of years . Master is good at making girls it seems " said Erika .

" That is interesting " said Diya lost in thought now . She would have to do some research on this and keep a eye on the devil . This 6th son thing did not sound like a good thing at all .

" I have to go meet her now . She

has no idea that she is alive . Master is tricky and has somehow made her believe she is dead " said Erika laughing as she walked out of the library .

It turned out that everyone that Diya asked in hell knew about the 6th son . She was shocked that somehow this piece of information had escaped her . She had found out that the devil had been married to many times to count . His last marriage surprised Diya as he had married a man named Teddy . She had seen Teddy in passing , never realizing who he was or that he had been married to the devil . This was a side of lucifer that Diya had not expected . His wedding was the buzz around hell . Everyone happy , except for Teddy it seemed .

Erika kept Diya updated on her day to day with the devils new wife , Joan . Apparently the devils new wife was not happy to be here in hell or married to the devil . Diya was not surprised by this news , who would be happy married to the worst man in history ?

Erika finally admitted to Diya that Joan was with baby , the demon in her could smell it . Erika had grown to like Joan and actually felt bad for her not telling her of her new pregnancy .

Now it did not come to Diya all at once , but more piece by piece . A plan was made . There was no way that Diya could let the devil have his 6th son . The more she thought about it , the more Diya was convinced that this was her destiny . To stop the devil from ruining all mankind.

She approached both Saphire and Erika about her plan , and to her surprise they agreed to help , no questions asked .

They all agreed they did not want the devil to meet up with his 6th son at any time at all .There was no guarantee that the devils wife would even have a boy , but that was not a chance Diya was willing to take . So a plan was made . They were going to help the devils wife , Joan , escape hell .

Blood moon was approaching fast .

It happened a couple times a year where portals

would open between upperworld and hell .

Believers of blood moon were devote devil

worshippers and that was the special time they

could pay homage to their leader , lucifer . Diya

thought it was silly and could not imagine praying

to the devil himself . Sometimes people would make

it through the portal , expecting to be welcomed by

Lucifer himself , some expecting praise or even

gifts for their devotion . Diya had witnessed it

several times and had a hard time not laughing at

the peoples reactions as they were thrown into the

depths of hell . When blood moon happened not

only could people come in but people could go out

as well . This is when Erika and Joan could escape

out of hell . Saphire had friends who hated the devil

and would be happy to help . She also found a spell

that would let Erika appear as a human . Erika at

first was unsure of the plan , once told that she

would be human , she jumped up and down in

251

happiness , agreeing right away .

Diya was thrilled everything was coming together so well . Erika , Saphire and Diya went over the plan daily . The day was fast approaching and Diya had been so obsessed with the plan she had forgotten one thing .

Where were they going to go once they escaped ? Diya froze . How could she not think about that ? They brainstormed for days and then Saphire jumped up with excitement .

" Paradise ! " exclaimed Saphire .

Erika and Diya looked at each other in confusion .

"Paradise !! It is a little village in the middle of nowhere !! It is a magical place . I went there years ago , children keep going missing there , a private investor hired me . " said Saphire .

" How does this help us ? " asked Erika .

" They can go there ! " said Saphire .

" Ok ... a place where children go missing ? Send a pregnant lady and a demon there ? " asked Diya .

" I will be human Diya " said Erika .

" I had a camp built for me outside of the village " said Saphire .

" Why ? " asked Diya surprised .

" Well I am a big deal ! I could not stay in the little village with those people . I had the camp built for me and my friends while we were there " explained Saphire as she twirled her hair between her fingers .

" You don't have friends " said Erika giggling at her own humour .

" Ha ha Erika " said Saphire sarcastically .

" Does it have water ? " asked Diya .

" It has natural hot springs , one of the reasons I built it there . When ever I need a break I go and hide there " said Saphire .

" How do you hide from the devil ? "

asked Diya .

"I put up a spell to protect the area from being found . Master does not need to know everything I do . " explained Saphire smiling .

"You are sneaky my friend " said Diya smiling back at Saphire .

"Yes I am " said Saphire .

Chapter 25

As luck would have it , the plan was set into action . Teddy the devils ex lover was angry about Joan and it was no secret . He had even went so far as to tell her about blood moon . This was also no secret as people in hell loved to gossip . He had been ranting and raving to whoever would give him a ear to listen . Diya had at first planned for Erika to convince Joan to use blood moon to escape hell , but Teddy had saved her that step . Erika at first upset , calmed down after Diya explained to her that this would work better and she would still get to be human .

" Joan wants me to take her to the records room tomorrow . I don't even know where this records room is ? " said Erika .

" The library Erika , it is sometimes referred to as the records room , you bring her to me " explained Diya . She was excited to finally meet Joan , 672th wife of lucifer .

" Oh ok " said Erika .

" Just do as she says . I will be here watching with the help of the Flora's " said Diya .

Erika did as asked and the next day the library door swung open and there stood Joan . She was around 5'7 , long brunette hair with bright blue eyes . Very pretty Diya thought to herself . Joan walked over to the desk that Diya was sitting at with wide eyes .

" Hello ? " said Joan.

" English ? " asked Diya .

" Yes ? " answered Joan .

" Well it has been a minute since I have spoken english . I am Diya . How can I help you ? " said Diya as she studied Joan .

" Hi , my name is " said Joan and she was interrupted by Diya .

" Joan , 672th wife of Lucifer "

" Hi " said Joan extending her hand
to shake Diya's .

Diya looked at Joan's hand .

" No , we must never touch . You
should be more careful . There are creatures down
Here that could really hurt you regardless of you
being one of our masters wives " explained Diya . It
was mostly true .

" Thank you " said Joan quietly .

A Flora flew down and whispered in
Diya's ear , Diya nodded and the Flora flew away.

" You want information on Blood
moon ? " asked Diya smiling .

" Yes " replied Joan .

" One minute " said Diya still
smiling . This time two Floras came to her desk and
she whispered in their direction . They both flew
off towards different parts of the dome .

" How did you know ? " asked Joan.

" Who you are or blood moon ? "

Diya questioned back .

" Both " said Joan .

" You are Joan . 672th wife of
Lucifer . It is my job to know . As for blood moon ,
the walls all have ears . You should be more careful
of what and where you say it . " exclaimed Diya .

" Fair enough . Can we keep my
visit to ourselves ? " asked Joan .

Diya looked up at all the flying
Floras in the dome and then back at Joan .

" I am not here to gossip but I cant
speak for everyone " said Diya looking back up at
the Floras .

" Thank you for your kindness "
said Joan .

The Floras started appearing and
dropping books on Diya's desk and flying back off .
Diya handed a stack of books to Joan and
motioned to a corner where there was another
stained glass lamp and desk , She reminded Joan
that the books stay in the library . Diya watched

As Joan sat down and started turning the pages of one of the books . Diya was overjoyed , the books Joan had been given should have all the information she needed .

Another book dropped out of nowhere surprising Diya . Looking around she could see no Flora in sight . It was a older book , leather cover with old yellow brittle pages . As Diya opened it she realized that this the missing piece she had needed to save hell . Hours went by before Joan finally got up to leave . Diya sighed a sigh of relief as she closed the library door . Gathering the book , Diya headed straight for the castle hoping Saphire was home , instead she found Erika at the front door .

" I have to bring Joan here " said Erika fustrated .

" Why ? " asked Diya .

" I told her that you and Saphire were witches " said Erika .

" Why ? " exclaimed Diya .

259

" She was asking so many questions . So I said you guys were witches and could help ? " explained Erika .

It actually worked out better . Erika brought Joan up to the castle . Saphire sat down with Joan all serious and then told her the truth . How she was actually alive , how her family had a generational curse and how Joan had been picked by Lucifer himself . Erika and Diya listened at the door . Saphire had made matching amulets for Joan and Erika to wear , keeping them connected and keeping Erika appear as a human . She also pulled out a pocket knife , marking both Joan and Erika with a symbol that would hide them from Lucifer . Diya gave Joan a letter , telling her not to read it until she reached upperworld .

Within days it was blood moon . Hell was a buzz of excitement . It was almost a holiday of some sort to the demons . Diya awoke excited as today was the day !! She waited patiently , re organized her room and then went for a walk . Diya's excitement turned to nervousness as the hours went by . Saphire had to ask a man named Preacher Mike to help Erika and Joan . She assured Diya he hated the devil more then she did and was happy to help with no questions asked . Diya believed Saphire but also knew it was hell and this Preacher Mike was not down here for being a honest man .

It was not until the next day that the alarms went off . Diya was sleeping and was awoken to the shrill sound. Wandering out to the kitchen she found Saphire standing with a smile on her face .

" It worked " whispered Saphire .

" It worked ? " whispered Diya back .

" The alarms have been set off which means master has closed down hell . Someone has escaped " said Saphire her dark eyes glowing .

Diya smiled and did a happy dance

In the kitchen . Saphire laughed at Diya .

" How long do the alarms go off for ? " asked Diya suddenly annoyed by the shrill sound . As if on cue the alarms stopped . The silence was deafening for a minute . Diya and Saphire stood there staring at each other for a minute before there was a loud knock at the castles front door . Both jumped in surprise .

" You going to get that ? " asked Saphire breaking the silence .

" Why me ? " whispered Diya . She was not sure why she was whispering .

" Fine . I will get it " said Saphire as she left the room to answer the door . She quickly re appeared with two demons . Diya stepped back in surprise and looked at Saphire confused .

" Masters wife and his demon are missing . These two want to search the castle . All of hell is being torn apart at the moment looking for the two . " explained Saphire as she smiled at the demons patiently waiting .

" Oh no ! By all means feel free to look where ever you would like . " said Diya to the demons . They thanked Saphire and Diya and left the kitchen to search the castle . Saphire gave a wink to Diya as she sat down at the kitchen table .

" Master must be livid " said Saphire .

" Has anyone else escaped from hell ? " asked Diya curious .

" Yes , there has been a few . Every couple hundred years someone gets brave . Blood moon has always been a escape route . Master is not dumb . He finds them right away and punishes them to the hell hounds . Nasty creatures . They end up living a life of being attacked and then eaten , over and over , no end to ever come . That is truly hell right there . " said Saphire the smile disappearing off of her face .

" I hope they are ok " whispered Diya . Erika was now a dear friend and she could not imagine what punishment would come to her if found.

Saphire and Diya sat at the table for just over a hour before the demons showed back up to tell them that their castle was clean .

" He wants to see you both " said one of the demons as they left the castle . Diya and Saphire looked at each other in panic .

" Of course " said Saphire as she closed the castles front door .

" Saphire ? " said Diya worried .

" It is show time ! He doesn't know , he wont know and if he does , we have a plan , right ? " said Saphire .

Chapter 26

Lucifer was beyond upset . He had his demons scouring hell looking for his missing bride . Saphire and Diya did as asked , both showed up to his office , wide eyed and appearing shocked to the news . He sat in his throne . It was made of skulls , all different sizes , stacked to make a massive chair . Beside him sat Teddy , all smiles and glowing happiness .

" Where are they ? " asked Lucifer angerly .

" How would we know ? " replied Saphire softly not looking up from the ground .

"How did you NOT KNOW ? " exclaimed Lucifer angerly .

Diya blinked and all of the sudden

Lucifer was standing directly in front of them .

Diya's eyes widened in surprise .

" My wife came to the library Diya .
What did she want ? " asked Lucifer in a calm
voice .

" Books on blood moon " whispered
Diya .

" Why ? " asked Lucifer .

" She was interested ? I have no
idea . I did not really talk to her . " replied Diya .

" Right " growled Lucifer as he
turned his attention to Saphire .

" Why were they at the castle
Saphire ? " asked Lucifer regaining his calm voice
once again .

Saphire looked at Diya quickly .

The room started to shake .

" Why Saphire ? WHY ? " yelled
Lucifer.

" Erika told your wife I could read
the future master . " whispered Saphire .

" And ? " growled Lucifer .

" She showed up at my front door so I gave her a reading " said Saphire .

" What exactly did you say to my wife ? Think carefully . " asked Lucifer again in a calm voice . Diya shivered , it was creepy how he went from intensely angry to peaceful calm in seconds .

" I told her of much happiness with being at your side master " said Saphire bravely .

" LIES " yelled Lucifer .

Diya shivered again at his sudden shift and the force of his voice .

" Maybe ask Teddy where your precious wife is ? " exclaimed Saphire .

" Oh really ? " said Lucifer calmly .

Lucifer turned to look at Teddy who was busy looking at his nails , unaware of the conversation .

" Saphire , darling , sweetheart . I need you to use your special powers , the ones I so graciously gave to you , to find my wife . " said Lucifer calmly still staring at Teddy .

" Yes master " whispered Saphire.

" And you " said Lucifer as if he was whispering in Diya's ear . She jumped and looked behind her , seeing no one .

" Diya . I do not trust you . It is nothing personal I am sure . I can not put my finger on it . Trust me I will find out if YOU had anything to do with this . " snarled Lucifer . Diya felt her hairs on her body raise in fear . She just stood there unsure of what to say . He had every right to distrust her .

" Now LEAVE ! I have other business to take care of " said Lucifer as he stared at Teddy .

Saphire and Diya quickly left the room . They walked in silence back to the castle .

The next couple months went by quicker then Diya expected . Lucifer moved his search to upper world , he swore to leave no stone unturned . He would find his wife . He hired

anyone and everyone he could find in pursuit .

Upperworld was his playground and he was

confident his wife would show up .

Erika and Joan barely made it to

Paradise . The occult shop that Saphire had taken

Diya to was attacked not even 24 hours after Erika

and Joan showed up .

Saphire suggested that they visit

Paradise , she had hired one of the locals to

keep a eye on things . Diya thought it was to risky

but Saphire assured her it would be ok , she would

keep them safe . Saphire grabbed Diya's hands and

the wind started to swirl around them .

" Oh you meant right now ? " said

Diya surprised .

" Keep your eyes closed " whispered

Saphire as the wind around them picked up . Diya

closed her eyes and felt the ground seem to fall

underneath of her . She grasped Saphires hands

even harder .

It could have been hours or minutes , again Diya was unsure of how long she had been holding Saphire's hands . All of the sudden the wind stopped and Diya felt her feet on the ground . She breathed in and it was fresh air , the sweetest smell she had smelt in years .

" You can open your eyes now " whispered Saphire as she let go of Diya's hands .

Diya slowly opened her eyes and was instantly blinded by the brightness of the sun . It took her eyes a minute to adjust . She looked around in amazement . It was a bunch of little cabins in the greenest pasture she had ever seen . They were surrounded by mountains , a little creek ran past her feet . What surprised Diya even more was her friends the Flora's . They were flying all around the encampment .

" Saphire , what are they doing here ? " asked Diya in shock .

" I honestly don't know Diya . They were already here when I got here . Floras live

Where ever they like . For some reason they live here as well . " said Saphire as she shrugged her shoulders .

Diya continued looking around the camp and noticed something else out of place . A huge white snake upon one of the cabins . It looked right at her as if it had something to say and then changed its mind and looked away .

" Is that a snake ? Just hanging out ? " asked Diya .

" That is Jess . She is with the Floras I guess . Can really talk up a storm " explained Saphire .

" The snake talks ? " asked Diya looking back over at the snake .

" Would you have it any other way ? She is very smart and keeps a eye on the Flora's and these hippies " said Saphire .

" I see " said Diya .

Saphire took her to a small cabin where inside she found Joan and Erika . Erika

Ran over and gave Diya a huge hug . At first Diya froze , she did not know the woman hugging her so tightly . Then she realized it was Erika in human form and hugged her back . It was a quick visit with Joan . Diya happy that she was all in one piece . She assured Joan that everything would be ok and took one last look around the little camp before finding Saphire to leave . Diya wanted to stay , in the sunshine , with the Floras and the people Saphire called hippies . But she feared Lucifer finding them there , with Joan . Diya said a prayer before grabbing Saphire's hands and disappearing into the wind swirl .

The next eight months dragged on . Diya felt as if time was going slower then normal . Lucifer grew angrier as each day passed that Joan was not found . Teddy stayed close to Lucifer , happy to have his lover back . Saphire kept a close eye on the little place called Paradise , reporting to Diya every week Joan's progress . Apparently Joan was growing very big and Erika was living it up as a human . Lucifer was determined and hired more head hunters to track down Joan . Diya was worried , she knew that everyone had a price , even the people called hippies .

Then all of Diya's worst dreams came true . Saphire came rushing into the library with a worried face . Diya instantly knew something bad had happened . Saphire never came to the library .

" What happened ? " exclaimed Diya .

" The camp was found by some head hunters ! Somebody had to have followed us . There is no way they found it on their own ! " said Saphire angerly .

" What about Joan ? " asked Diya .

" I told you I hired someone to watch over them ? Her name is Jen , she has taken them and hidden them in a cave up near the camp . She called me as soon as this went down . Jen says that Joan is ready to have her baby and

that she will keep me posted . I can not chance
going there in case master shows up . " explained
Saphire .

        " I feel so useless " whispered Diya.

        " I trust Jen . Joan and Erika will
be fine . I am going to find out who has their nose
in our business ! " said Saphire angerly as she
turned and walked out of the library .

Chapter 27

Days went by without any news . It
was silent . Finally Saphire losing patience agreed
with Diya , they had to go to Paradise . Diya eagerly
grabbed Saphire's hands , not sure of what to
expect on the other end . It was the same as
before , swirling wind , the ground disappearing
and then silence . The smell hit Diya before she
could open her eyes . She knew it well , it was
death . Opening her eyes Diya could see why .
Bodies were everywhere , dead , rotting in the sun .
The smell was over whelming and unexpected .
Diya and Saphire searched the little encampment ,
then the caves up above . They found evidence in
one cave of childbirth , towels with blood , but no
Joan or baby to be seen .

" Who did this ? " asked Diya as they walked back down from the caves .

" Master . He was here " replied Saphire .

" So he has Joan and baby ? " asked Diya sadly .

" No I do not think so Diya . Master would have sounded the bells of hell in victory . It is silent in hell ." said Saphire who seemed to be deep in thought as she spoke .

They returned to hell at a loss as to what had happened . It was only a couple of days before Saphire came rushing into the library again to Diya's surprise .

" Any news ? " asked Diya hopefully .

" It was that sneaky bastard ! He just could not keep his nose out of it ! " said Diya angerly .

" Who ? " asked Diya excited .

" Teddy ! " exclaimed Saphire .

" Teddy ? How ? " asked Diya in disbelief .

" One of his servants told me . He has been bragging all around . Teddy followed us to Paradise . " explained Saphire .

" So does he have Joan and baby ? " asked Diya .

" No . Well yes . Get this . Joan had two babies . " said Saphire .

" Two babies ?! " exclaimed Diya loudly .

" A girl and a boy ! " whispered Saphire looking around the library .

" Where are they ? " asked Diya .

" Joan escaped with the baby girl and I have been told Teddy has the boy " said Saphire .

" Where is Teddy ? " asked Diya almost shouting .

" His servant told me she has been going back and forth to this place called Valhalla .

It is a mountain range with a series of caves . Blood moon members use it for sacrifices . " explained Saphire .

" He is going to kill the baby boy ? " exclaimed Diya in a panic .

" No , worse yet . He is going to give it to Master for a gift " said Saphire .

" That can not happen " said Diya again almost yelling .

" Calm down . I have set a plan into action Diya . Without you everything as we know it would be dammed for eternity . I did not sign up for that my friend " said Saphire .

" Without you as well " said Diya.

" I have been listening to the air waves of hell and picked up a call the other night . I hope you do not mind but I said I was you . It was Joan , I told her to go to Vahalla . " explained Saphire .

" Why ? " asked Diya now really concerned .

" Because if we go running in to take the baby , Teddy will out us right away and open masters rath . Erika and Joan seem to have a lot of help . I am not worried , Erika has been waiting to tear Teddy's head off since the first day they met . I also set up a cabin and left a encouraging note from you , again it was short planning but Joan trusts you Diya . " explained Saphire .

" You have been busy " said Diya .

" I had no choice . Time is ticking " said Saphire with a serious tone .

" You know we are going to have to use our back up plan . Lucifer will never stop looking for his children . " said Diya .

" It has no guarantee Diya " said Saphire with a worried look .

" If we don't try , we will never know if we could have stopped all of this ." said Diya .

Saphire frowned and nodded at Diya in agreement .

Diya could barely sleep , eat or function . She was worried about Joan and the babies . If the devil reunited with his son , it would be the end of everything she loved so dearly . Diya had never prayed so hard for anything or anyone . It was hard not to feel useless , she was stuck in hell while Erika and Joan were fighting for their lives in upper world .

Saphire had lost all contact with the servant who had been reporting to her . She had been unable to find out anything for a day and was starting to freak out .

" Maybe we should leave Diya " said Saphire as she paced back in forth frantically .

" Have faith " said Diya . Although she was having a hard time as well , not knowing was agonizing .

" Faith ? " exclaimed Saphire .

" It will work out . I just know it . " said Diya . She was trying to stay positive and take her own advice .

With Diya's last word the bells started ringing throughout hell . Diya's heart fell . The devil was back and the ringing meant he was victorious . Diya held back tears as her eyes watered up .

" We have to try " whispered Diya .

" We can still run " whispered Saphire while trying to smile .

" We have been running our whole lives . It is time to stop . " said Diya .

Saphire's dark eyes let one single tear roll down her tender cheek and drop onto the floor .

" You are right " said Saphire .

The bells stopped ringing and a loud voice announced that everyone was requested at the great hall . Diya looked at Saphire and grabbed her hand for re assurance .

Hell was more lively then Diya had ever seen it . People , demons and everything else that lived in the pits were making their way to the

Great hall . Excitement was in the air like electricity . As Diya and Saphire got closer they had to push their way through . Rumours flew through the air like birds . By the time they made it to the entrance they had heard many speculations . One lady stopped to tell Saphire that the devil had found his wife and baby , another that he was unable to find his wife and was setting the hell hounds lose on upperworld and her favorite so far , the devil was beheading his ex lover Teddy . Diya's mind was so confused after hearing so many stories .

Saphire pulled Diya through the crowd and ended up in front of a stage . Diya looked around , the hall was packed full and was starting to smell like death mixed with feces .

Music started to play loudly . The lights changed to swirling spot lights . Diya watched as Lucifer entered the room from the ceiling . He swooped around the hall with wings wide open . Demons cheered the loudest and

flames shot up from the ground . Lucifer flew
around the hall cheering on the people before
gracefully landing on the stage . He raised his
hands and the hall went crazy , exploding with
noise . Diya thought for a minute her eardrums
were going to explode . Saphire gave Diya's hand a
squeeze and she nodded . Lucifer lowered his
hands and the hall went quiet .

" THANK YOU " yelled Lucifer .

The hall gave a quick cheer and
then went silent , waiting on Lucifer's orders. He
smiled and then snapped his fingers . Erika and
Joan appeared on stage next to him . Erika back in
her demon form and Joan who looked like she had
cried a million tears . Where were the babies ? Diya
looked at Saphire in confusion .

The crowd started chanting .

" KILL KILL KILL "

" I have a problem " said Lucifer to
the crowd of people . They went silent , waiting for
the devil to continue .

" I have found the TRATOR and my mislead wife . " said Lucifer .

The crowd cheered .

" I am offering a reward for whoever finds my children . A reward that has never been offered before , a seat next to me , for eternity . " said Lucifer .

Before Diya knew what she was doing she jumped up on the stage and threw a 3 of spades playing deck card at the devils feet .

" TRINTY ! " yelled Diya .

Chapter 28

TRINTY

When 3 magical individuals , one of
magic , one of demon and one of pure heart , come
together to imprison pure evil . The pure of heart
must throw a 3 of spades at the pure evil . The
three must come together , joining hands around
said evil and chant .

The great lord hath sent me

He hath added his pure spirit to mine

He hath added his pure voice to mine

He hath added his pure spittle to mine

He hath added his pure prayer to mine

Whether thou art a evil spirit , evil demon

Or a evil ghost or a evil devil

Or a evil god or a evil fiend

Be though removed from me !

By heaven be thou exorcised !

By upperworld be thou exorcised !

May the fever , pain , sorcery and all evil

Be removed from the body of the wanderer .

The chosen three must chant this three times , circling said evil . If all works properly the evil will leave the body and into the trinity box .

The trinity box is made from a blessed oak tree with specific directions as to what time of year and day .

The Flora's had dropped a old leather book on Diya's desk when Joan made her visit to the library . Upon further inspection Diya realized it was a book of old spells and incantations . She could find no date , time or even indication of where or who the book had come from . Diya did not even know if the book told truth or was just for entertainment . It was all she had that gave her hope .

Diya had been studying and waiting for this day to come . She hoped that she was pure enough of heart to make this all work . Saphire and Erika would practice with her day in day out , until they all felt like they knew the chant without fear . It was fun at first but it came with a lot of seriousness . The three of them knew if it did not work , they would all be tortured for eternity .

TRINITY

The card fell in front of Lucifer's feet , 3 of spades looking him in the eye . At first he looked confused and then started to laugh .

Saphire jumped up on the stage and grabbed Diya's hand , before they knew it Erika joined them in hands . The three stood back , holding each others hands , making a perfect triangle . Lucifer stood in the middle laughing .

The three started yelling the chant , holding onto each other for dear life .

" STUPID WITCHES " yelled Lucifer over their chant .

The hall was silent . Everyone watched in amazement as no one had ever seen the devil being challenged before . A scream could be heard as Teddy came running onto the stage towards the ladies . Out of no where Joan came running and tackled Teddy down to the ground , fists a swinging . Teddy turtled , yelling for help .

Diya held on tight as they started the chant a second time .

" YOU ARE NOTHING BUT DEVIL SPAWN " growled Lucifer . He tried to move but his feet were acting as if they were rooted to the stage .

" YOU ARE GOING TO PAY FOR THIS ! STUPID BITCHES ! LET ME GO !! " yelled Lucifer as he tried to jerk his feet from the floor . He tried to extend his wings but they were no longer there . His eyes widened in amazement and he grew even angrier .

" Stop now and save yourself Saphire darling . You know you are special to me " said Lucifer in a sweet calm voice .

Diya squeezed Saphire's hand and Saphire gave a squeeze back . The three finished the chant and started for the third time , this time really yelling it out .

" STOP THEM !! " screamed Lucifer as he looked around the hall . No one came to help . It was as if they were hypnotised by the ladies and the chant .

Teddy started to get up from the ground , in a effort to help the devil . Joan quickly kicked him in the face , leaving him laying unconscious on the ground . People around her cheered as he hit the ground , some patting her on the back . Teddy did not have many friends in hell it seemed .

As Diya , Saphire and Erika finished yelling the last line of the chant , Lucifer went silent and dropped to the floor in a motionless heap . They stood there , holding hands , looking down at the body laying on the floor . The blessed oak box made a loud click . Looking over Diya could see the lock had been set .

Shock set in and then then the three of them started jumping up and down in excitement . They had done it ! They had locked up Lucifer . The hall was silent . Demons stood in shock and were unsure of what to do . Whispers started everywhere . Joan ran up to the stage .

" What just happened ? " asked Joan .

" We locked up Lucifer " answered Erika as if it was a everyday thing .

" Where are my children ? " asked Joan looking at Diya .

" You don't have them ? " exclaimed Diya in surprise .

The ground started to shake and it was as if the ceiling cracked open . The brightest light Diya had ever seen started shining through the crack in the ceiling directly onto her . Diya was over come with warmth and the feeling of love . She let herself fall in the light as it carried her up towards the ceiling . Diya was hanging 20 feet in

the air when she exploded into a million stars . It

was as if fireworks had gone off , shooting stars as

far as the eye could see .

" What the hell ? " said Saphire in

amazement .

" Where did she go ? " asked Erika

in disbelief still looking around for Diya to

reappear .

" I don't know " replied Saphire

sadly .

" What did you do to Diya ? " asked

Joan as she walked over to Lucifer's body and

kicked it .

" She will be back " said Saphire as

she walked over and picked up the blessed oak

box .

" How do you know she will be

back ? Diya just exploded all over hell ! " exclaimed

Erika still wide eyed .

" She is my best friend . Diya will

come back . I just know it . " replied Saphire .

" I hope so " said Erika .

The great hall was full of noise now , all of hell did not know what to do without their leader .

" GO BACK TO WORK ! " yelled Joan at the crowd of people suddenly with a anger that Erika had never heard before .

Chapter 29

Diya awoke , laying in a green field with blue shy above , sun shining in her face . She sat up quickly and then sat back down feeling out of place . Then she noticed her arms . They had no markings on them . Diya quickly checked herself over to find not one mark on her . At first she was sad as she had gotten used to her special marks .

" Hello ? " whispered Diya to the empty field .

" My child " responded a voice that seemed to come from everywhere around her .

" God ? " asked Diya surprised . She looked around but could see no one .

" Yes my child " responded the voice .

" Why can I not see you God ? "
asked Diya .

" My light would blind you "
answered God as smoothly as a song lyric .

" Why would you never let me die
my lord ? I begged and begged . You never
answered " cried Diya . She had been waiting for
this day for over a thousand years and now it was
here .

" You needed to experience
everything to make you the one you are today my
child " answered God .

" I am a ABOMINATION ! " cried
Diya feeling all the pain of her life at once .

" There are no abominations my
child . I have made every living thing for a reason ,
even demons have a purpose . " explained God
with the sweetest voice Diya had ever heard .

" Am I a demon ? " asked Diya in
surprise .

" No my child " answered God .

" You are one of my angels sweet Diya " said God .

Diya was speechless . A angel ? She had never thought of herself as a angel . All of this time she thought of herself as a mistake . Diya sat in the green field in silence trying to comprehend what God had just told her .

" You are one of my chosen few Diya . You are the light . You are the pure at heart . You needed to understand why humanity needed saving " said God reading Diya's thoughts .

Tears ran down Diya's face . All this time she had been questioning god , not understanding he had a plan for her , from the start . She was not a abomination , she was a angel . Everything suddenly made sense . Every moment , the sadness , grief , happiness , loss and joy . Everything in Diya made sense at that moment and she knew where she belonged . A sweet breeze touched her cheek as she fell back down to lay on the green grass .

Saphire paced back and forth in her castles kitchen while Erika watched patiently .

" I cant not find Diya ! I can not find the babies ! Hell is coming unhinged !! " exclaimed Saphire in a panic .

" It will be ok " said Erika calmly .

Saphire stopped pacing to look at Erika .

" No it is not ok ! I am losing my mind ! How are you so calm ? " whispered Saphire with frustration .

" I just have this feeling . I just know everything is going to be ok " said Erika smiling .

" I don't think Diya is coming back Erika " said Saphire sadly as she sat down at the table next to Erika .

" Why not ? " said Diya as she walked into the room .

Both Saphire and Erika jumped up from the table in joy , running over to hug Diya .

296

" Where have you been ? " asked

Erika .

" What happened ? " asked

Saphire .

" I have found the babies " said

Diya, changing the subject .

" Where ? " asked Saphire and

Erika at the same time . They looked at each other

annoyed for a minute before looking back at Diya

for a answer .

" Jill had been talking to a boy for

months on the internet . He convinced her to take

the babies so they could have their own family , I

found them in Italy . Safe and sound . Jill handed

them right over without a argument . To be honest I

think she was happy I showed up . She looked

exhausted . " explained Diya with a twinkle in her

eye .

" So where are they now ? " asked

Saphire .

" They are to be raised in a church .

Joan should be arriving to be with them at any moment . I will supervise them always . " explained Diya .

" Where did you go ? You blew up in a million pieces and have been gone for weeks " asked Saphire .

" Heaven " answered Diya .

" What ? " said Saphire in surprise .

" You went to heaven ? What was it like ? " asked Erika . Saphire looked at Erika and rolled her eyes . Erika's tail started to sway in annoyance .

" What happened to all of your markings on your arms ? " asked Saphire looking at Diya closely .

" Are you even Diya ? " exclaimed Erika taking a step back .

" Those markings were incantations to keep my truth hidden from Lucifer " said Diya .

" What are you ? " asked Saphire .

" I am a angel " amswered Diya .

" No way ! " exclaimed Erika wide eyed looking at Diya as if seeing her for the first time .

Saphire stood staring at Diya , arms crossed .

" What are you doing here then ? " asked Saphire frowning .

" I am here to run hell " answered Diya smiling .

" Are you serious ? " asked Saphire as she started to smile .

" Very Serious " answered Diya.

" Can I help ? " asked Erika .

" I will need both of your help " said Diya .

It had been Diya's choice . God had offered her a place in heaven . Diya at first overjoyed grew silent and lost in thought . As the days went by she came to realize that heaven was not her home . Nothing was familiar . It was beyond beautiful and almost to perfect . Diya missed hell .

She missed Saphire and Erika . She missed the library , her castle , even the demons with the bad jokes . Hell had been the only home she had ever really known and she had grown comfortable there . God had told her she could have anything she wanted , so she asked to take over Lucifers position and run hell . God did as she asked .

And Diya did run hell . She did it with a firm but fair hand . Diya ruled with respect not fear . It was not a easy feat . Saphire and Erika helped a lot . Diya did not like to punish anyone , unfortunately there were those who demanded punishment as if they were thirsty for it . Diya kept the balance between heaven and hell . Praying every night for guidance .

Now that Diya thought about it . This was probably Gods plan all along .

Many are the plans in a
person's heart ,
But it is the Lord's
purpose that prevails

Proverbs 19:21

32438079R00166